The Erthod
De Groai Fad
{The Uniting Call}

WRITTEN BY:
Anita E. Shepherd

ILLUSTRATED BY:
Victor Saenz

To my family of the
Universal Elven Society

~ PROLOGUE ~

At one time, the universe was a living structure. Every planet, solar system, galaxy, and star lived in an abundance of light and was continually self-sustaining. There were five major planets that were most important because they fashioned the elements of nature. From these five planets, other smaller planets were derived all over the universe.

There were beings who inhabited the universe at the time, the Living Elemental Elves or the LEE. Full of light, energy and life, they dwelled on the planets to maintain and nurture the elements for all to enjoy. The LEE wore a colored leaf that represented their home planet connecting them to the elemental qualities; blue for water on the planet Nen, yellow for prairies on the planet Laer, green for forest on the planet Nimloth, white for mountains on the planet Tinc, or red for the desert on the planet Naur. It was not so much to diversify them, but to allow them to channel the strength from the elemental planet when needed. The LEE were very mystical but their power was part of their existence allowing them to perform their sacred duties in nurturing life and light.

The universe was home to many other beings as well, some who had developed their own way of controlling elements through magic: the Witches, Warlocks and Wiccans. For eons of time, everyone lived in unison but slowly the Witches and Warlocks began to develop great pride in their accomplishments. They believed themselves to be better than the LEE and were convinced in their minds that they should be the ones to rule over lands and elements within all the worlds. However, their spells altered the elements from their natural state into what they deemed more superior. The catastrophic changes caused the LEE to intervene, but the Witches and Warlocks refused to comply with their orders and caused great strife between them. The Wiccans, however, stayed true to their calling and stood with the Elves. The resentment taking hold within the Witches and Warlocks gave rise to jealousy and they revolted against the Elves and Wiccans.

Thus, a mighty Chaos War took place throughout the universe. Life began to be destroyed upon planets and the blasts from the battle created deep scars within the stratums of the cosmos. It seemed as if the war would be lost by the Elves and Wiccans. However, another group of beings that hailed from worlds within worlds came to their aid: the Druids. The Druids were warriors who stood for truth and honor. Their kingdom was centrally located in one realm where they lived and fought as one body of power.

The Druids helped to turn the tide of the war in favor of the Elves and the Wiccans, but the damage to the universe was already done. In an effort to preserve the original state of the cosmos, the Elves, Druids and Wiccans compelled the war to one location in order to trap the dark forces. On the east side of the universe, a planet had not been damaged yet and all of the elements were still working in harmony; its name was Erthod. There was no habitation outside of nature and its animals on Erthod, so they set a hard course there.

Prologue

The Druids, Elves and Wiccans drove the Witches and Warlocks to one spot within the darkest, coldest part of the world: the Dark Crystal Caverns. Known as the Abandoned Ones, they were banished to spend their lifetimes exiled from the Light of the Living for their rebellion against the LEE.

Knowing that the destruction in the universe from the Chaos War would soon follow them to Erthod, the remaining LEE Zoetial, or High Elven Elders, sacrificed the Gift of Light within themselves to create a protective shield around Erthod to keep it from being demolished. It was to be a place where all of the living could continue and thrive.

The war had a devastating impact on the lives of those who fought and many were lost to its grueling combat. Once established on Erthod, a great council was held and a pact was made between the remaining Elves, Druids, and Wiccans. The society of the universe would live on in this world, everyone dedicated to their own purpose and station.

Of the Lee Zoetial who had sacrificed themselves, there were five princesses who were appointed rulers of the elemental regions on Erthod to maintain the virtue of the lands. One Enchantress for each element: Arathron of the Mountain realm, Elorah of the Forest realm, Valentia of the Plains realm, Norin of the Desert realm, and Oceanna of the Coastal realm.

Arathron's father was the Master of Swordsmen who had taught Arathron how to be one with the metal of the lands. She had grown to be strong and steadfast in all she did. It was clear she was destined to be Enchantress of the Mountain realm. With her positional duties upon her, Arathron proved to be very refined in the element of the precious living metals and understood the importance and beauty the mountains had to offer. Arathron was respected in all the lands, and all that inhabited the mountain realm honored her. She was usually seen taking long walks with the snow leopards but loved to fly in the skies atop the great sorni, or eagle.

Elorah's parents were the high ranked keepers of the sacred living trees and were masters of Pilinge, or flight of the arrow. She was very passionate and protective of the forests. It was agreed that with her skills, she would be the most successful as Enchantress of the Forest realm. She dedicated herself to nurturing every plant, creature and atmosphere that dwelled within the woodland regions and everything returned her dedication with great homage. Elorah's most favored animal was the Olympic Elk with whom she journeyed the forests many times throughout the days. In the evenings, she was usually found walking among the tree branches surrounded by fireflies.

Valentia was a bit younger than all the other princesses, but was wise in discovering living elements in flat new regions resulting from land changing events. She had learned this from her father who taught the skill of Yaavan, or harvesting. Valentia was very attentive to even the smallest of detail and found happiness when witnessing new life emerge through tumultuous habitation. As Enchantress of the Plains realm, Valentia knew that unity always brought forth peace. Those that were entrusted to her care had the greatest of faith in her rulership. Valentia loved being out in the openness of the Plains as it was a symbol of truth and honesty. She enjoyed watching the butterflies and the variety of animals and plant life thrive around her.

Norin was a born leader as her father was a great Commander in the Sun Army. She grew up training alongside him as he persistently practiced wielding his fiery staff. He was stationed most of the time where the worlds' suns were the strongest. With her knowledge of the arid habitat, she was chosen as Enchantress of the Desert realm. Norin focused night and day on the different levels of heat and how to resolve what creatures and plant-life could survive the best way. Norin was known to be very intuitive and charming, for it was in the desert where she learned to discover beauty and wisdom beyond what the eyes and senses could find.

Of all of the elements, water was thought to be the most dynamic as it borders the edge of chaos and order. Oceanna's parents both served as Elven sea rangers and utilized the trident as an armament that enabled them to both calm and upset the element as needed. Oceanna and her brother travelled the coastal waters of every world with their parents and became the most accomplished Elves with the trident. She was taught to be observant yet free in order to move with the ever-changing currents. Oceanna was chosen as Enchantress of the Coastal realm with her brother as her protector. She was known throughout all the realms as one of mystery, beauty and determination; reflecting the living quality of the realm she oversaw.

On Erthod, the Enchantresses became known as the FLEESE: Five Living Elemental Enchantress Sister Elves.

~ Chapter One ~

It was a time of agreed peace among the five Elven elemental realms. Now, by agreed peace, it means that as long as the Elves stayed within their elemental regions, there would be no hostilities among them. One might ask why there was such disharmony. Some would say it was caused by their constant disputing regarding which element was more powerful. At one time, they all worked in unity, with no divisions. But since their arrival and control on Erthod, they lost sight of the importance of their roles within the world.

The competitive nature among the Elves reflected in the elemental regions they were entrusted to rule over. The Mountain and Forest Elves contended against one another as to which element deserved to be the most majestic in height; and so the trees were constantly being strangled out by the stony, metallic minerals, while the mountain sides were cracked continually by the trees trying to push upward through the stone.

Another conflict was between the Coastal and Desert Elves, constantly debating which would be the most sustainable for the world; therefore, waters would thrash upon the arid lands causing floods, resulting in dry heat waves pushing the ocean waters to recede drastically from the shorelines.

The Plains Elves usually tried to be neutral in all the disputing by exhibiting that all can reside together and thrive. They maintained one spot on Erthod as an example, known as the Waterfall of Paluok. However, common ground was never found among all of the Elves and it was decided all would be best if left to tend after itself as separate regions. It wasn't perfect, but it worked, for the most part.

The Druid domain was situated within a valley that was only reached by passing through the Gates of Marana. Within their kingdom of Wringastol, they had Ovates who were the most revered among all Druids because of their skills of prophecy and divination. However, there was only one Ovate who remained since the Chaos War, his name was SkyLar and he had the link to all those who had been before. The Druids remained a peaceful people, but of course they were not strangers to war. Not just anyone could pass through the Gates of Marana to reach the Druid Kingdom, for they revealed the intent of the heart and mind. If proven worthy and favorable, the gates would be forgiving and allow passage. But if proven to hold wickedness within the bowels of the soul, the gates would send one to his or her fate of damnation.

The Elves and Druids had no dealings with each other and kept to their own as it was against sacred laws within both circles to mix outside the bloodlines. But one day, a child was conceived of an Elf Prince named Tolgin and a Druid virgin priestess, Reya. Their union, of course, caused great discord among the two groups. Tolgin was stripped of his honor and banished to the Dark Crystal Caverns, a place reserved for all the evil darkness. It was a place of desolation; a dungeon beneath the earth.

Chapter One

Reya was sent to isolation within the Druid temple to have the child. When the child was born, she was a baby girl of great shame as there was no place for her at all. The Druids vowed to offer the baby as a sacrifice for Reya's iniquity, and so the child was placed upon a flat stone on the edge of the forest that bordered the Valley of Pumthale, outside the Druid Kingdom, where she was left to suffer her fate. Reya's contempt for the Druids' decision regarding her child drove her away and she was never seen again.

However, another domain was established on Erthod; it was the Wiccan Enclave known as Fyecshain. The Wiccans were peaceful and devoted their lives to magic of the natural realms and how to excel in their abilities. Some Wiccans mastered moving in instant flight of travel, some to foretell the future, and some simply how to use the gifts within nature for healing. The Wiccans practiced within their own domain, but had recently begun fighting an evil in other dimensions. They believe the evil is being brought by the Witches and Warlocks. Although the Witches and Warlocks were physically banned to the Dark Crystal Caverns, they had been striving to pierce through on the unseen level. Yet, the Wiccans had been counter-spelling their deeds to keep them at bay.

So on the fateful night of Reya's baby being placed for sacrifice, a ceremony was underway in the nearby Wiccan village. They were all gathered around a great fire when water fell from the sky and smothered the flames, except for one spark. It lingered in the stillness of the air and moved slowly through the trees, as if it was beckoning them to follow. A few Wiccans felt the call and pursued the spark, where it led them to the baby. They could see that she was an elf by her ears; however, when the spark landed on the baby's arm, it revealed a birthmark of Druid lineage. The birthmark was that of four circles with one circle in the middle. The Wiccans recognized it as the elemental five-fold symbol. They realized then that the five elements had protected the child and knew she must have a higher purpose. They took the child in among them to raise her until her path was revealed. They named her Asvoria.

Asvoria grew older and came to know that her lineage was mixed between the Elves and the Druids. Beyond that, there was nothing that could be told to her except how she was found. Overtime, she was imparted with visions and the Wiccans were very attentive to her gift to help her cultivate it for the purpose she had.

As she mastered and became one with her calling, Asvoria's visions began to lead her to provide advisory messages to the five Elven realms and the Druids. Knowing there was some unpleasant past in her life with the Elves and the Druids, the Wiccans arranged to have a private messenger communicate Asvoria's visions to the FLEESE and to SkyLar, the Druid Ovate whom they esteemed as the Solitary One, for he was often found alone as he dedicated his life to the prophecies revealed to him.

Asvoria was never seen by the Enchantresses or the Druids; howbeit, they referred to her as tungol, meaning wise. Her visions were always welcomed as they guided the Elves and Druids with forewarnings through difficult occurrences among them. But what Asvoria didn't know yet, was that her path was one of an even greater destiny. For it was she who held the very prominent and important position of connecting the Elves to the Druids in a soon to be revealed time of trouble.

Asvoria loved to spend her evenings studying the stars. The nebulas, the constellations, the planets and star clusters all had a story to tell and seemed to portray what she believed to be signs of events that happened in the past, present and will happen in the future.

Chapter One

On one particularly clear night, Asvoria went to her favorite spot on top of a rock that was nestled at the edge of the trees. It was the rock she was found upon by the Wiccans, though Asvoria wasn't aware of that. She only knew she was always drawn there when she would get a vision. As she sat down, Asvoria pulled the hood of her brown cloak back, revealing her golden chestnut colored hair that fell across her shoulders. Her long, flowing dress draped around her.

The air was unusually still this night. As she studied the stars, she had a most disturbing vision of a great battle. She saw the five Elven realms surrounded by a large army comprised of groups that she had never seen before. They were terrible to look upon; grey and deathly. There seemed to be three divisions led by what looked like Elves, but these Elves were dark and fierce. Nothing like the Elves Asvoria had known of in Erthod. The army closed in around the Elves and she cried out, pulling herself from the vision. It took a second for her to remember where she was. Her heart beating rapidly, she sat still and looked around her into the night. She wondered when the vision would take place, if it would it be soon.

Asvoria slowly walked back to the Wiccan village and contemplated about when she had her first vision in regard to the Elves. She knew little about her heritage or who her parents were. The Wiccans seemed to keep most of it a secret except the fact that they had found her. They explained her life with them as a gift and responsibility for the world, but she never questioned beyond that. *Why was that?* she thought to herself.

When her visions about the Elves began, she had been introduced to Tavol, a Wiccan who had mastered the flight of swift travel and could move instantly from place to place through a portal he had created with a spell. It was he who would go to the Elves and the Druids to relay Asvoria's messages. It was all very mystical to her and yet her mind and soul grew more at peace with her calling upon receiving each vision.

What Asvoria pondered now in her thoughts as she grew closer to Fyecshain, was why her visions had always been about the Elves and the Druids, but this evil that was coming seemed only to be upon the Elves. What was even more disturbing to her, were the others in the vision whom she had never seen before.

As she arrived at the village, she sat down by the central fire. It was custom for her to go here after she saw a vision while others would gather to listen. But tonight, she was silent and it was apparent to those nearby that something was wrong.

"Asvoria?" a gentle voice called her out of her thoughts. She glanced up and saw Esme looking at her with concern. Esme had been the closest thing to a mother to Asvoria and the only one in whom she could confide in. Tonight, however, she didn't have the words to describe what she saw.

Esme sat down next to her and took her hand. "What did the vision show you tonight?"

Asvoria quietly studied Esme's face. Her weathered skin and caring eyes stared back at Asvoria expectantly. Returning her gaze back to the fire, Asvoria said quietly, "Something terrible."

Esme squeezed Asvoria's hand tighter and said, "You need to speak the vision aloud. Terrible or not."

Asvoria looked around the fire and noticed that others had gathered to hear. The crackling from the fire seemed to hush itself in an effort to receive what she was going to say. She took a deep breath and said, "I saw a great and dreadful battle. The five Elven realms were surrounded by a deathly and evil assembly of beings that seemed to look like Elves. The others among them were groups that I haven't seen before."

"These others," Esme started, "Can you tell us anything more about them?"

Asvoria thought back to the details, "They wore a mark on their foreheads."

There was a quiet gasping that went through the air from the group. Asvoria looked at Esme, "What does it mean? Who are they?"

"These are the Abandoned Ones, the evil Witches and Warlocks that always plague the spirit world that we are mingled with," replied Esme with uneasiness. "They dwell in the Dark Crystal Caverns. For many years they have been silent among the spirits, but we didn't know why. We knew they must be conjuring something and we have used this space of time to do what good we could. It was during this time that we found you."

A voice from across the fire spoke, "You must tell the Elven Enchantresses." It was Myrrden, a quiet but strong Wiccan esteemed by the village. He would often times come to the fire to hear Asvoria's visions, but would never say anything. So tonight when he spoke, it was a notable alarm.

Asvoria's voice trembled timidly as she responded, "How can I speak this evil vision of doom to the Elves without offering a recourse of help?" She looked around the fire and asked, "Will you aid them in this battle?"

There was silence as everyone just stared at the fire. It was almost as if no one heard what she had asked.

"We don't fight outside the spirit world," Esme finally stated as she broke the silence.

"But the marked Witches and Warlocks are of the spirit world," Asvoria implored. "You said that yourself."

"Yes," Esme replied, "but we can't help the Elves in *this* world."

Myrrden stood up and as he turned to walk away he replied, "You know the ones who can help."

Asvoria sat in silence for a second, frantically thinking of someone who would go to the Elves' aid and then knew of whom he spoke. "The Druids?" she whispered intently with a furrowed brow.

As she looked up, she noticed Myrrden was no longer there, as well as others who had took their leave of the fire. She felt Esme stand up, and quickly grabbed her hand. Esme gazed down at her with pitying eyes.

"How can I convince the Druids to stand by the Elves?" Asvoria questioned. "I don't know what to say to them. You know as well as I that they have no dealings with each other. Would they yet go into battle together because I come with a vision?"

Esme gave her a sad but encouraging smile. "Don't forget who you are, Asvoria," she coaxed. "It is your destiny."

Asvoria shook her head in frustration. "Ugh, my destiny," she stood up in exasperation, throwing her arms in the air and began to pace by the fire. "What does my destiny have to do with this horrid battle about to take place?"

Esme walked over to her. "Why do you like viewing the stars so much, Asvoria?" Esme asked as she adjusted the edging of Asvoria's cape around her shoulders.

"I've always been drawn to them," Asvoria answered looking up at the night sky. "There's something about them and the universe. I feel they're trying to tell me a story."

"Yes," Esme said as she lifted her eyes up to the stars. "There is a great story. What you see is the after effects of another great battle that took place a long time ago."

Asvoria studied Esme curiously and asked, "A battle long ago? Between who? The Elves?"

Esme returned her gaze to the fire, nodding her head. "And others. It was the Great Chaos War."

"Did the Wiccans fight?" Asvoria probed further, coming in closer to Esme.

Esme drew in a soft breath answering, "Yes, and we thought we did everything we could to keep another battle from happening," Esme replied, "But it would seem as if what we did wasn't enough."

"How did you think you resolved another battle from happening?" Asvoria inquired.

Esme looked at her, "We drove all of the evil into one place, below the surface, banishing them from the light. It was to be their prison until they all died off, never to be seen again."

Asvoria's eyes squinted as her eyebrows scrunched towards each other, her frustration turning into resentfulness. "If the Wiccans fought then, why not fight now?" Asvoria prodded. "I don't understand, it seems as if you should be taking part in this."

"Our part of your journey here on Erthod was to take you in and nurture you until your appointed time of purpose," Esme explained. "The Wiccans all knew this. Now your purpose is laid out in front of you. You must heed to it." Esme cupped Asvoria's hand in hers. "You must go."

Asvoria dropped her head a little as she slowly understood what Esme was saying. "You're telling me that my time among the Wiccans has come to an end."

"I'll have Tavol come to you," Esme said as she released Asvoria's hand and walked away.

Asvoria was left alone by the fire. Her thoughts raced inside her tired mind of how she was to take on this great task. *It's my destiny?* She thought to herself and sat down on a log.

"Well," she spoke aloud to herself, the fire being her only audience, "if it is my destiny and purpose, then it will be accomplished." She raised her face up at the stars, closed her eyes and said a silent prayer for strength and guidance. She didn't hear the approaching footsteps but suddenly felt a presence nearby. Opening her eyes, she saw Myrrden standing in front of her.

He spoke in a low but confident tone. His dark hair laid long across his shoulders. "I've brought you something," he said as he extended his hand. Asvoria stood up and opened her hand to receive his offering. Myrrden dropped a white stone in her hand saying, "The white Moonstone carries the energy of the new moon at its height."

"It's beautiful," Asvoria said in awe as she held it up to the moonlight. The pearly veil of the stone seemed to open up to the light, reflecting its silvery-white line across the surface. "It's as if it holds a mystery."

"Yes," Myrrden replied. "Its secrets are locked within. As with your own inward journey, Asvoria." Asvoria looked at him as he continued. "And with your own light, those secrets have been brought to the surface to serve their purpose."

Asvoria sighed, closed her hand around the Moonstone and looked down at the fire. "It's been such a peaceful time here among you. I've learned so many enchantments. Now I'm to head into an unknown part of my journey alone. It seems now is when I need the strength of friends."

Myrrden turned to go and said, "You'll never be alone, Asvoria. Just as the moon seems to be alone in the night sky sometimes," he stopped, looked up and continued without turning back to Asvoria, "there are always stars nearby." He glanced over his shoulder toward Asvoria, then walked off into the night.

Asvoria watched as Myrrden's broad stature disappeared, remembering what he said, "The white Moonstone carries the energy of the new moon at its height." She looked again at the Moonstone and then up at the moon. "Four days until the new moon," she said aloud. "My 18th birthday."

"Asvoria?" a familiar voice sounded behind her. It was Tavol. His modest stature and long, brown hair would be an engraved memory in her mind. He gave her a small, brown satchel. "Esme wanted me to give this to you."

Asvoria took the satchel and peeked inside. It was filled with fruit and bread. Shrugging her left shoulder, she smiled at Tavol. "I guess this will be our last mission together," she spoke kindly.

"I will deliver this one last message with as much honor as I have delivered all the others," Tavol pledged, returning the grin. He gave her a folded paper. "You'll need this as well."

Asvoria opened the paper and saw that it was a map to Wringastol, the Druid Kingdom. She chuckled a little. "Thanks, Tavol."

"I figured since you'd never been there before, it might be helpful to know where you're going," Tavol advocated.

"Yes. Well, I guess the best place to have everyone gather would be where all the regions converge," Asvoria said. "So, just let them each know to meet me at the Waterfall of Paluok by tomorrow's sunset."

Tavol nodded, turned around and departed through the portal of his flight of travel.

She surveyed the village of what she could make out by the light of the fire. Pulling the hood of her cloak over her head, she started on the passage towards Wringastol.

And so began the next phase of her journey.

~ Chapter Two ~

The FLEESE all reside in their specific elemental realms. Each Enchantress has a personal high ranking Mihman, which is an Elvish guard. The Mihman have one duty, and that is to protect their Enchantress. No one comes near the Enchantresses without their approval. It is the Mihman that Tavol usually meets with when he comes with a message from Asvoria. He has never met the Enchantresses personally.

Elorah's realm of the forest is where Tavol's task led him to first. Elorah has many small divisions of Woodland Elves throughout all the forests on Erthod, but her main refuge is called Metasequendron. Built among the tallest redwood trees in the western hemisphere, Metesequendron can hide itself from peering predators with ill intent. It's one of the most peaceful places on all of Erthod.

Elorah communicates with all of her Elves around Erthod by sending messages upon the wind through the trees. This keeps her messages safe from anyone else who may try to interfere.

Elorah's chamber is housed in the top central portion of Metesequendron, with branches that surround the sides creating a sanctuary of her own. She usually rests peacefully, but on this night, she did not. An unusual dream awoke her.

"Are you okay, Enchantress?" Lotriel asked Elorah as she poured water from a pitcher by the bed into a cup created by the forest leaves. Lotriel is Elorah's first hand assistant. She hummed a mystical tune summoning for some fireflies to come into the chamber and dispel the shadows. In an instant, the room was illuminated by tiny, blinking lights dancing around.

Elorah sat up staring into the night sky through the opening above her bed. "A warning was given to me this night," she said, stepping out of bed. "I must go to Dolu."

"Dolu is down with the Nightwatch," Lotriel reminded with caution while assisting Elorah with her dark, green cloak.

"Yes, I am aware," Elorah said. "I need to be there as well. I believe we may have company soon."

"Shall I go with you?" Lotriel asked. She reached over on the table nearby and handed Elorah the Leaf of Nimloth to clasp her cloak together. This is the leaf worn by all Woodland Elves.

"Not right yet," Elorah replied and gave her a smile. "Let us see first what this meeting will be. If I need my bow, I'll send for you to bring it."

Elorah walked over to the window and spoke to the trees in a gentle manner, "Besar fadu." A wind began to blow and rustle through the leaves. She pulled her cloak hood over her head and stepped out onto the wide branch just outside her doorway. The branch's leaves embraced Elorah like a protective wall as it lowered her down to the ground below.

✥ ✥ ✥ ✥ ✥ ✥ ✥ ✥ ✥ ✥ ✥ ✥

It was still before daybreak as Tavol arrived, stepping out of his portal within five miles of Metasequendron. As he neared Elorah's refuge, he could see the dim lights of the fireflies that surrounded the entrance way to the main quarters, peeking out in the distance.

He was halted by a small group of Elven guards. One stepped forward with his bow crossed in front of him and his hand ready to reach for arrows. Of a tall and imposing stature, he seemed to loom in front of Tavol.

"Dar!" the guard commanded Tavol to stop.

Tavol bowed his head, bringing his arms out of his cape and held them straight out at his sides to show himself to be of no harm.

Just then, Tavol heard a familiar voice offer him the Elvish phrase of peace that he had heard many times in coming to Metasequendron.

"Ton ri dug, Tavol." It was Dolu, Elorah's high ranking Mihman. He was of mid-height but seemed taller with his broad shoulders held straight as he stood at attention in front of Tavol. He held a large oak bow with an image of a halo surrounding a tree on the upper tip.

Tavol looked up and returned the greeting, "Ton ri dug, Dolu."

Dolu turned to the other guard and said, "It's okay, Aranel. He's a friend."

Aranel relaxed his stance and stood at attention behind Dolu.

"You'll have to forgive Aranel," Dolu said respectfully to Tavol, "he has just been promoted to Captain of Honor and has not been familiar with our meetings."

Tavol smiled and said, "All is well, Dolu. I have a message from Asvoria."

Dolu nodded solemnly, "Yes of course, what is the extent of the message?"

"It is more of a request this time," Tavol responded.

"Request?" Dolu replied and crossed his arms. "There has never been a request from Asvoria before. Please state the - ". Dolu stopped and listened to the wind in the trees. He returned his gaze to Tavol and squinted curiously.

Tavol stood anxiously waiting to hear the message Dolu heard. He could tell by Dolu's austere expression that it was something of an uncommon nature.

"She is on her way here," Dolu stated in a guarded tone. He quickly shot an arrow into the upper branches of a tree. At once, there was an army of Woodland Elves at the trunk of every tree surrounding them.

Tavol sensed the immense reverence that was around him and suddenly became apprehensive; both with the knowledge of meeting an Enchantress for the first time and that this may be his last time in the realm.

Suddenly, the sound of galloping filled the air and as it drew closer, one could make out the silhouette of a hooded female rider atop an impressively large beast with a massive antler rack. The Woodland Elves nearby emerged bowing their heads. Dolu drew near to the beast, which was now revealed to be an extraordinary Olympic Elk. Dolu held his arm out for Elorah who dismounted and pulled her dark green hood back. Her deep brown eyes and hair seemed to shine through the darkness in the forest.

This was Elorah's first time being in the presence of anyone outside of the elves. Her heritage had taught her to always be protected and allow others to go before her in all she does. However, with the warning she was given, she knew she must hear the messenger's words herself.

Elorah glanced towards Tavol and spoke in Elvish to Dolu inquiring if he was the messenger. Dolu nodded and replied, "Yes, Enchantress. O prag Tavol, un Asvoria."

Elorah graciously walked towards Tavol and met him with a smile. Tavol bowed his head.

"Ton ri dug, Tavol," Elorah greeted. Her voice was calm and youthful.

Tavol looked up and beheld her sweet and simple beauty. He replied courteously, "Ton ri dug, Enchantress."

"I have heard many good things about you from Dolu," Elorah continued. "Your wise one has provided us with countless beneficial assistance through her visions."

"Asvoria is a kind soul who only wishes to fulfil her purpose among you," Tavol stated, surprising himself with how calm he was in Elorah's presence.

"I know this is quite unexpected for me to be here, but it came to me this very day in a dream that I just awoke from, that a messenger would bring important news of my realm," Elorah said. "We honestly don't have any messengers enter our realm except you, Tavol."

Tavol nodded as he sensed even more the great importance Asvoria was to the Woodland Elves. "Yes, Enchantress," he said.

"However, Asvoria has not sent me with a specific message but rather a request for you to meet her at the Waterfall of Paluok by today's sunset."

Dolu, filled with eager vigilance, stepped forward and quickly responded, "No, the Enchantress meets no one outside of her realm."

Elorah turned to Dolu and held her hand out as if to quiet him, "It's for my realm that I must go."

Dolu took a deep breath and whispered with caution, "Enchantress, we have never met Asvoria personally, not even I." He straightened his shoulders and offered in a stern, yet respectful tone, "Allow me to go in your stead. You remain here in protection."

Elorah's eyes glistened with determination. "I will go," she replied conclusively, "and you will accompany me."

Dolu sighed feeling nothing but uneasiness. He turned his eyes to the ground in dissatisfaction, perpelexed at the situation that he had never been faced with before. His place had always been in front of the Enchantress in everything. Protecting, guarding, shielding, teaching, and advising. Now, for the first time, he felt conflicted about his role. He contemplated within himself, *Prevent her from going? Dare override her orders?*

Elorah could sense Dolu's internal struggle and touched his arm, trying to ease his uncertainty. "Don't let this turning of the great story cloud your mind to what has been written for you to undertake. I too am journeying beyond what I have always known in duty." A smile crept to her lips as she raised her eyebrows in a mischievous manner. "Besides," she teased, "perhaps I will finally get to put all that training to use should anything come against us."

Dolu raised his head a little and remarked, "That is not funny, Enchantress. My training for you has its place but not for you to bring the danger to yourself."

Elorah noticed the deep concern in Dolu's eyes and responded in Elvish for him to rest his mind, "Gim hal, Dolu. This meeting has been designed for a purpose that has called to me."

Dolu gave a sober nod. Not comfortable with the thought of Elorah making the journey, his concern was somewhat eased knowing he would be by her side to protect her.

"Funod. Bav ye ton," Elorah said to Tavol, thanking him and bidding him to go in peace.

As Tavol disappeared into the forest using his flight of travel, Elorah turned to walk back to the elk. Dolu came in step beside her and spoke with apprehension in his voice, "I have to tell you, Enchantress, that as much as I want to carry out your request, the burden of caution lays heavy on my shoulders."

"I know, Dolu," Elorah replied as she stopped by the elk and grabbed ahold of its thick mane. She paused for a second before climbing up on the elk's back and stated, "But there is something to heed when you're warned in a dream." Elorah climbed up onto the elk's back and adjusted her seating.

Dolu's voice was fraught with urgency as he lent his hand for a step, "This is the first time you have met with anyone outside of Elven lineage. First Tavol and now Asvoria."

She looked around at the trees and said, "I have a feeling that today may be the beginning of many firsts and lasts." She gave Dolu an understanding glance, pulled the hood of her cloak over her head and stated, "Lotriel will bring my bow." She called out a very melodious hooting sound and a spotted owl flew from a nearby tree toward Metasequendron. She looked at Dolu and asked, "Shall we go then?"

Dolu turned to Aranel and instructed, "Send your best Normi to scout ahead."

"Brug ri peon, Normi Hav!" Aranel commanded as he looked through the surrounding forest. It was his command to the Elite Scouting Group, to take to the trees for Enchantress protection.

In unison it was heard, "Meurti!" The Normi Hav did what they do best and hid themselves within the branches of the trees. Some closer, some further away, providing a vast expanse of protection.

Lotriel arrived swiftly on an Okapi with Elorah's bow and handed it to her. Dolu looked up at Elorah and she nodded. He then started out on foot in front of the elk. Lotriel fell in line behind Elorah's elk. The fireflies lit up the way through the forest as the trees pressed back their branches to form the path of Sleonma, also known as the Way of the Woods.

~ Chapter Three ~

Aruonta is known as the DayRiser Mountain range in the farthest point east, for it is here where the sun first greets the new day. Covered with fresh snow every morning, it is where Arathron's day begins reminding her that she must always maintain the pureness of heart. It is on top of the mountains that she feels the lightest, enjoying the freshness of the cool breeze on her face. This is her most treasured place, and if she could, Arathron would pause the moment and bask in its glory forever.

Being Enchantress of the Mountain region, Arathron has the tremendous responsibility to ensure all is well among everything that dwelt therein. It could be a difficult task to stay in tune with the ever changing terrain, so Arathron carries her sword at all times. The sword had been forged deep within the caves of Ravan, where the mountain core is the strongest. The pommel of the sword holds an embedded amethyst; for it is the amethyst that is the hidden source linking all the mountains together, carrying the strength of Tinc. When the sun's rays shine upon the amethyst, it reveals to Arathron if there is trouble anywhere in the mountain region. Though for many, many years the amethyst has always reflected perfectly in the sun's light signifying the peacefulness of her reign, Arathron always carries out the task with devotion.

On this day, as Arathron stood on the highest peak of Aruonta, she moved closer to the edge, her white dress flowing under her silver, velvet cloak with the current of the wind. The thick snow crunched under her feet as she walked on top of it, not sinking into the element but as if it was frozen water. As the sun awoke from its slumber, Arathron pulled her sword from the sheath on her hip and raised it to the sky. Just as had always been in times past, this day's sun shone brightly onto the amethyst revealing serenity in the region.

While she was putting her sword away, Arathron heard a screech in the distance. She turned to the west and could see a great golden eagle flying toward her. The screech of the eagle holds many meanings for Arathron and signals to her messages from Polodren; Arathron's Mihman, who is also her cousin. Polodren has served by Arathron's side since she became Enchantress. There is no one she trusts more, yet sometimes his jesterly ways are found to be out of place.

As the eagle flew and landed on her arm, Arathron stroked its feathers. "Good morning, Beleg, my noble friend," she smiled. "What news from Polodren do you have for me this early in the day, hm?"

The eagle screeched quietly and tapped its claw once meaning that Polodren had beckoned her to the tower of Ofunar, which was situated in the side of Ravan Mountain and overlooked the greater part of the Mountain region from the highest point. Ofunar is Arathron's dwelling and where her elite army resides.

Arathron paused for a moment, breathing in deeply to take in the solitude before responding to Polodren's request. The breeze was subtle as it wisped her long, white hair across her forehead. Longing to stay a little longer, she knew it was time to go. Arathron blew on the eagle and as it spread out its wings, lifting up from her arm, the eagle grew to five times its size. It landed gracefully and stretched its wings down so Arathron could climb on top.

"Bav rund, Beleg," Arathron said summoning the eagle to fly swiftly. She patted Beleg's head and he flapped his majestic golden wings. He released one resounding screech that seemed to shake the mountains, indicating to the mountain region that Arathron was in flight.

Soaring through the crisp mountain air atop Beleg, Arathron surveyed the region. Her keen eyesight allowed her to see down to the streams that flowed through canyons, creating their own special paths. She loved flying close enough to the mountain sides so she could view the caves where some of her most magnificent animals dwelt. And as Beleg glided by, the animals emerged from their dwellings to pay homage to Arathron.

As they grew close to Ofunar, Arathron observed Polodren standing at attention on the high tower. Polodren held out his hand to Arathron as Beleg flew low to where he was standing. Arathron took his hand as she dismounted. She turned around and blew on Beleg once more. Flapping his wings, Beleg returned to his normal size and perched himself on the stone banister that wrapped itself around the edge of the high tower.

"Thanks for coming so quickly. Nice hair by the way," Polodren playfully stated glancing up at Arathron's wind-blown look. As they began to walk together along the tower terrace, Arathron laughed a little and smoothed her hair down, pulling it behind her left ear.

"Well what is so important that you beckoned me so early?"

Arathron asked.

"We have a visitor. But, first," he stopped her, "I need to give a little background before we continue."

Arathron tilted her head a little to the side and replied, "Polodren, are you playing a trick on me? I've already met with the sun and there are no problems in the mountain region."

"Not a joke, Enchantress," Polodren said. "This visitor, Tavol, is one I greatly respect as he is the one who has always brought Asvoria's visions to us."

Arathron glanced toward the tower entrance and pulled her hood over her head. "Can he see me?" Arathron responded cautiously.

Polodren touched her arm prompting her to look at him. "Yes," he said, "but it's okay. Belaraniel is with him in the conference hall. He has a special request from Asvoria this time and I thought perhaps you would want to hear it yourself."

Arathron unsheathed her sword one more time holding it up to the sunlight, but didn't see anything unusual reflecting in the amethyst. She nodded at Polodren assenting to see Tavol.

As they walked through the entrance tower into the conference hall, Belaraniel cleared her throat and Tavol stood very still and quiet. He bowed his head as Arathron drew near. Belaraniel was the Strategic Griunk, in charge of preparing the animals for traveling.

"Tavol," Polodren announced, "This is Arathron, Enchantress of the mountain region."

"Ton ri dug, Enchantress," Tavol replied looking up at her face. He was astounded at the beauty Arathron held. Like Enchantress Elorah, she possessed a purity and sweetness, yet Arathron seemed to have a strength in her eyes.

Arathron was surprised at Tavol's knowledge of the Elven greeting. "You know our language?" she asked.

"Just what is necessary," Tavol responded humbly.

"Polodren has informed me that your wise one has a request of me." Arathron asserted with a glance toward Polodren.

Polodren regarded Tavol, signaling him to speak the request.

"Enchantress, Asvoria has requested that you meet her at the Waterfall of Paluok by today's sunset," Tavol stated.

"Meet her?" Arathron enquired uncertainly. She turned to Polodren and requested with a forced smile, "Can I speak with you for a moment?"

Polodren cleared his throat, "Yes, Enchantress."

As they stepped outside onto the terrace, Arathron sighed and asked, "Need I even query how you would advise me on this request?"

"I don't feel a threat," Polodren replied. "You know if I did I wouldn't have even let him speak to you." Polodren's face displayed aspects of wanting to say something more.

Arathron noted the hesitation and bid him to continue, "Jevas, Polodren."

Polodren exhaled, groaning a little, "Tavol has told me that this request was for all the Enchantresses and that he has already spoken to Enchantress Elorah. She is already heading to the destination."

Arathron turned to survey the mountains as she thought about the likely tension that would be generated among them all. "It's been awhile since we have all been together," she declared. "You'll be going with me," she commanded.

Polodren nodded, "Of course."

"We will take the wolves," Arathron instructed as she adjusted her hood.

Polodren nodded again, "Of course. Don't want to arrive disheveled."

Arathron could see Polodren's playful smirk. She relaxed a bit, nodding her head to consent to Asvoria's request. They returned to the room where Tavol was waiting patiently.

Arathron smiled warmly at Tavol for she knew he must have been a little uncomfortable with her earlier reaction. "Thank you, Tavol," she said. "We will heed Asvoria's request."

Tavol bowed his head and took one more look at her engaging eyes before turning to leave.

"I'll see you out," Polodren said to Tavol as he looked at Belaraniel and instructed, "Prepare the wolves." He then addressed Arathron and spoke in Elvish, "Fa nuon, Enchantress."

Arathron replied with a small smile to let him know she would be mindful of his guidance and not be fearful of the venture ahead.

As Polodren and Tavol headed out of the tower, Belaraniel also bid her leave from the Enchantress and departed out the side corridor of the tower that led to a high staircase to the grounds below. She stopped at the top, whistled in a high yet peaceful tone to call the wolves in, and then began her descent down the stairs.

Polodren and Tavol walked down the corridor stairs toward the entry of Ofunar. As the stairway ended, Polodren stopped and bid Tavol farewell, "Bav ye ton, Tavol."

"Bav ye ton, Polodren," Tavol returned the farewell and moved to take his flight of travel. As the portal came into view, Tavol took a step toward the opening, but was knocked backward to the ground by an invisible force.

Polodren quickly came to his aid to help him up. "Are you alright, Tavol?"

Tavol shook his head a bit and stared straight forward, trying to detect the force that interrupted his magic.

"Polodren?" came a soft voice from the side corridor, belonging to Luthien. She was a young Faordun, which is the middle stage of a mountain Elf reaching their highest potential. Luthien still had her full red hair, which wrapped in toward her face. Wisps of white emerged throughout, signifying that she was transforming into her completeness as a high rank. Her green eyes were fixed on Tavol with an intense gaze.

Polodren noticed the uncharacteristic look on her face. "What is it, Luthien?"

Luthien was hesitant at first but began to slowly speak. "A strangeness came over me just now. I'm not familiar with it. And I thought I saw...," Luthien stopped and slowly walked closer to Polodren.

Tavol stood up and urged Luthien firmly, "What did you see?"

"I'm not sure," Luthien replied with a worried expression.

Polodren touched her shoulder and felt her shiver slightly.

"Luthien...," he said calmly, as he could tell that she was extremely shaken.

"Whatever it was, I felt it," Tavol said. "And if my thought of what is happening is correct, then I must hasten my steps as quickly as I can to meet with the other Enchantresses before sunset. I expect my flight of travel will be hindered along the rest of my mission."

"Bav rund, Tavol," Polodren encouraged him to go swiftly.

Tavol gave a firm nod and ran with quick resolve toward his next location. Polodren turned his attention back to Luthien, searching her eyes. They were dark and deep with concern. He took her by the hand to lead her up the stairway to Arathron.

As they reached the top of the stairs, Luthien pulled her hand back from Polodren and stopped. "I don't want to tell the Enchantress what I think I saw," she whispered.

"So tell me," Polodren entreated, "for certainly whatever you think you saw, whether it be real or a trickery, had a tremendous effect on you."

Luthien stared down at her tightly clenched hands. "The banished prince," she said as her voice trembled a little.

Polodren's breath caught in his throat. For a few seconds, without breathing or speaking, he tried to think of how this could be possible. "Are you sure?" he asked finally.

Luthien nodded her head in silence. Polodren moved closer to the archway into the tower chamber where Arathron was, then stopped.

"You may come or go," he said gravely. "But this will need to be shared with the Enchantress."

Luthien quietly asked, "I...I just...," her voice trailed off, then she regained her composure and continued, "I just don't understand why I would see such a thing. Why me?"

Polodren replied, "I don't believe it's coincidence that this happened today. This much I know." He sighed and ran his fingers through his hair. "I would request that you come with me though. The Enchantress may be able to ease your troubled spirit."

Luthien agreed to go with him. As they walked through the archway, Arathron was staring at her sword. She turned her gaze to them, dropping her sword a little.

"Something is wrong, isn't it?" Arathron asked. "I felt the power of Tinc from the amethyst for the first time call to me, as if in warning."

Polodren approached Arathron, leading Luthien by his side. "Enchantress, there came a disturbance just now that affected Tavol's flight of travel. Something hindered him and knocked him to the ground."

Arathron pulled her cloak hood back and queried, "Is Tavol harmed?"

"No," Polodren answered. "He quickened his steps to his next destination since he will be on foot. He said he thought he knew what the disturbance might have been, but..." he paused in his sentence.

"But I saw something, someone at the time Tavol was affected," Luthien added, her voice stronger and no longer shaking. She suddenly felt a sense of predestined purpose in what took place, though still not sure why she was the one to witness it.

Arathron's expression grew extremely guarded. "Someone?" she questioned.

"Yes, Enchantress," Luthien replied.

"Who was this someone that you saw, that was hidden from the vision of others?" Arathron asked as she began to pace slowly, still holding her sword and looking at the amethyst.

There was a short space of silence, then Luthien responded, "The one who was banished."

Arathron stopped abruptly and her eyes darted to Polodren. Polodren slightly lifted his chin to indicate that he believed Luthien.

"It can't be," Arathron stated in alarm, "He was banished to the Dark Crystal Caverns with the Evil. Never to be let loose. Never to rise from the darkness."

"Well, I don't know how, but it would appear that the darkness is moving itself up," Polodren said.

"That just means," Luthien stated, "that the Light will rise higher, right?"

Arathron turned and gazed out the archway that led to the tower terrace and replied, "Yes, Luthien. The Light always rises higher." She slowly started walking to the terrace. Polodren and Luthien followed behind her. "But never without a fight," she ended her sentence with finality.

"We'll be ready," Polodren said fervently.

"Will we?" Arathron asked as she slid her sword into its sheath on her side. She pulled her cloak hood over her head. "Perhaps this is what the meeting is about that Asvoria has called us to." She stopped at the banister and breathed in the fresh mountain air.

"Belaraniel will have the wolves ready. I'll summon the Tugeom ready for departure at once," Polodren stated.

Luthien stepped forward, "Enchantress, I'd like to go as well."

Arathron turned to look at her and said, "Yes, Luthien. I believe you may be needed on this journey. For some reason you were able to see the banished. It would appear that you have a gift of dimensional sight."

"Is that why I was able to see him?" Luthien asked. "I've never had that happen to me before."

"Some are gifted with certain abilities for specific seasons," Arathron replied. "It appears that your season is now."

~ Chapter Four ~

As Asvoria neared the Gates of Marana that opened to the Druid Kingdom of Wringastol, she suddenly felt very fatigued in her body and mind. She tried to press further knowing that her time was limited in order to get to the Waterfall of Paluok by sunset, but it was if all of her strength was being drained from her.

She sat down on the ground under a tree to eat a little of the food Esme had packed for her. As she opened the satchel, she drifted off to sleep in spite of her efforts to stay alert. Immediately, she found herself somewhere she had never been. It seemed real and Asvoria felt a pressing force to be at peace, yet she was not settled inside. *Was she dreaming? Was she in a trance?* Asvoria couldn't tell.

She appeared to be in a place where things were reflecting like a maze of mirrors. She could see herself partly in the mirrors in a hazy fashion, as if she was a mirage staring back; however, there were holes where her eyes should be. It started to become cold.

"Asvoria."

The mention of her name was like a whisper she could hear, but yet a call in her head.

"Asvoria." The voice came again.

She looked around but saw no one. She didn't recognize the voice. She attempted to walk yet found her steps to be heavy as through thick mud. As she pressed through, her movements became petrified and her chest began to feel cumbersome. She was becoming frantic.

"Who's there?" Asvoria called out with what air she could muster in her lungs, but there was no answer. Her voice echoed through the reflecting glass and resounded back to her own ears as a deafening sound.

"Asvoria. You're not worthy." The voice grew louder, penetrating into her.

Asvoria suddenly became aware a female figure standing on the other side of the glass. It was not a reflection of herself, it was someone else. She tried to step closer, but the figure disappeared. She reached out to touch the glass and it suddenly transformed to water. She searched for something to grab on to as the water rose quickly all around her.

"Wake up, Asvoria!" she told herself. "It's not real! Wake up!"

She felt as though she was trapped in this realm and couldn't get out. Just then, she heard another voice calling her name, "Asvoria!"

This voice she was akin to and she called out, "I'm here! I'm here!"

She tried to move her body outside of the realm, trying to wake herself up by a jolt. With the water rising almost up to her neck, Asvoria tried to splash with her arms, anything that would cause a motion big enough to throw herself out of the sleep.

Just as the water was about rise above her head, she felt a hand reach down and grab her arm. Someone was trying to pull her up, but the water was causing her whole being to be immovable. Asvoria attempted to stretch with all her might and press towards the direction the hand was pulling.

"Asvoria, fight!" the voice demanded. "Use the stone!"

Asvoria took a deep breath and with every ounce of strength she had within her, began to kick her feet to loosen the grip of the mire that held her captive. She reached into her pocket for the moonstone that was given to her. Once she had it in her hand, she screamed and felt a burst of light shoot from her soul. In that instance, she awoke.

Breathless and stunned, Asvoria looked around and saw Myrrden kneeling beside her holding her arm. She held the moonstone in her hand.

"What was that?" Asvoria asked him. "Where was I?"

Myrrden sat back on the ground beside her. "You were being attacked by a Lajak."

"A what?" Asvoria exclaimed and began to stand up.

Myrrden took her arm and helped her as he stood up as well. "A Lajak," he said. "It's a defeating spell that tries to keep one trapped inside their own mind with no hope, strength or power."

Asvoria shook her head, "But I don't understand. I was fine. I just felt a little tired. Where did it come from? Where did you come from?" She looked at him with an expression of both confusion and wariness.

Myrrden adjusted his cloak and answered, "I've been following you since you left the village, just to make sure you would be okay." He motioned in the direction of the Gates of Marana and nodded, "Also, to make sure you could get through."

"Why wouldn't I get through the Gates of Marana?" Asvoria asked following his motion with her eyes toward the Druid Kingdom.

"Only those who are found worthy are allowed to pass through," Myrrden replied. "Otherwise the result is fatal."

Asvoria inquired, squinting her eyes at him, "Why was I not forewarned about this?"

Myrrden stated in his deep, resounding voice which seemed to bring both a peace and anxiousness to Asvoria, "We knew you would get through as long as you held onto nothing that would cause inhibitions."

Asvoria glanced toward the ground, "Inhibitions. You mean to make me think I'm not worthy?"

Myrrden nodded and slightly turned his head as he looked at her eyes. "Do you have doubts?"

"Well, I didn't," Asvoria scoffed as she threw her ams in the air in dismay, "until I was just attacked."

"And why would that make you doubt?" Myrrden asked.

"Well, a voice told me I wasn't worthy," Asvoria stated, her voice cracking slightly as she held back tears.

Myrrden said nothing but just kept his gaze focused on her. Asvoria looked away and said in a frustrated tone, "Maybe I'm not."

"Was it your voice you heard?" Myrrden questioned, keeping

the same intent stare.

"No," Asvoria shook her head and looked back at him. "I didn't know this voice."

"Then why listen to it?" Myrrden queried.

Asvoria considered that she had never felt fear before and knew then that it only comes from doubting one's self. She took a deep breath. "I understand."

"Someone, something is trying to keep you from fulfilling your purpose. That should tell you that you are on the right track and that you are worthy." Myrrden explained. "Know yourself, Asvoria. And don't forget what you know. It's all inside of you. You can't lose it. Because it is you."

Asvoria smiled at him, "Thank you, Myrrden." She fixed her cloak hood on her head and began to start walking. "Will you be joining me the rest of the way? I only ask because you can walk beside me and not in the shadows."

Myrrden returned her smile saying, "It would be my delight to travel with you the rest of the way to the gates; however, you must go to Wringastol alone."

Asvoria nodded her head. "I shall enjoy your company while you are here."

Just then they heard a rustling noise from a nearby bush. Myrrden held his hand out signaling to Asvoria to stay and cautiously moved closer to the bush to investigate. He bent down and quietly grabbed a stick. When he got close enough, he quickly and decisively jabbed the stick into the bush.

"Ow!" cried a high pitched voice from within the bush and out fell a young man with sandy blonde hair that stood out around his head like tiny spikes.

"Jofmed." Myrrden stated dryly and crossed his arms as he towered over the young man.

Jofmed scrambled to his feet, straightening his cloak and belongings that were in a state of disarray. He cleared his throat and waited for Myrrden.

"What are you doing here?" Myrrden queried sternly.

"Wait, I've seen you around the village," Asvoria said.

Jofmed smiled wide and announced, "Yes, I'm Jofmed!" He spoke quickly and his eyes twitched a little when he smiled.

"We know," Myrrden retorted, "the question remains as to why you are here?"

Jofmed stumbled over his words as they came quickly pouring out without thought, "Well, you know, I was, I was walking along this here path, and – um – well, I was … shocked beyond surprise when I saw Asvoria! And so I said to myself that I wouldn't be much of nothing if I didn't at least come and say hello...," he paused, looked at Asvoria, and said, "Hello!" He waved, laughing nervously.

Asvoria tried to muffle her laugh. Myrrden rolled his eyes and said, "Asvoria, this is Jofmed. He's my initiate."

"Hello, Jofmed," Asvoria greeted him with a smile.

"You need to head back to the village," Myrrden instructed.

Jofmed's face dropped and his shoulders slumped. Asvoria felt a little sorry for him and asked, "Can't he come along?"

Myrrden peered at her with narrowing eyes. Jofmed raised his eyebrows at Myrrden with a pleading expression. Myrrden relented with a crooked smile.

"Fine," Myrrden resolved. Jofmed hopped with excitement. "But no magic unless I authorize it." Jofmed nodded his head vigorously. "And," Myrrden continued, "no lagging or getting too far ahead." Jofmed continued nodding his head, the smile on his face growing wider. Myrrden looked at him and just shook his head.

"You know where we're going, right?" Asvoria asked him. "This isn't a fun adventure."

"Oh yeah, sure," Jofmed agreed as he adjusted his cloak. "The Gates of Marana where you'll be found worthy or become deceased right there on the spot and …"

"Anyway," Myrrden interrupted him. "We will travel with Asvoria to the Gates of Marana but not inside the Druid Kingdom."

"Right!" Jofmed exclaimed standing straight and tall with a quirky smile on his face. "Ready!"

As they started walking, Jofmed asked, "Um, so did anyone bring anything to eat by chance? I am soooo hungry because, see, I left without packing any food. Well, I packed food, but ate it already because," he paused and laughed, "see, I didn't realize how long we were actually going to be gone and…"

Myrrden opened his pouch and threw a loaf of bread at him. Jofmed caught it just as it hit his chest. He gestured with gratitude and ate it in silence as he followed behind them along the path.

As they walked along, Asvoria asked Myrrden, "How did you know that I would be attacked?"

"Your mission is one of great importance, Asvoria," Myrrden started, "I'm not sure you quite understand that yet."

"Well, I'm trying to," Asvoria explained, "but I just learned about the Great Chaos War. It would seem there is so much that happened in times past that I know nothing about and yet those events are playing a big part in what is happening with me now."

"It's true that what happened before played a role in what is now unfolding," Myrrden explained, "but because of what happened then, you are able to now do your part and help those who need it."

"How come you never spoke to me at the village until now?" Asvoria asked.

"It was never needed," Myrrden stated. "I'm not much for idle talk; conversation should have purpose in it."

"That is so true," Jofmed mumbled as he took a bite of bread.

Myrrden glanced slightly over his shoulder at him. Asvoria chuckled and then let out a slight gasp as they reached the top of a hill. Before them stood the Gates of Marana, exceedingly tall and shiny silver in color. A symbol of a tree was engraved over the place where the gates met together.

"I guess this is it," Asvoria said with a weak smile.

"What does the tree symbol mean?" Jofmed asked as he finished the last bite of bread.

Myrrden answered, "It represents the Druid tree of Life."

"Which explains the fateful decision for those who try to enter," Asvoria stated thoughtfully.

Myrrden put his hand on her shoulder and reassured, "No doubts. Should trouble find you on the inside, you now know the power that the moonstone holds. Don't be afraid to use it."

Asvoria clutched the moonstone in her pocket. "I won't."

"We'll be here when you come back," Jofmed smiled and looked at Myrrden, who shot him an irritating glare. "Won't we?"

Asvoria smiled, took a deep breath and turned to walk toward the Gates of Marana. As she stepped closer, she closed her eyes and held on to the words of Myrrden, clearing her thoughts of everything except of what she knew in her heart. Asvoria heard the gates unlock, but she didn't open her eyes, she just continued moving forward. She felt the earth shake under feet as the gates opened, allowing her to enter. She couldn't understand it, but she felt a sense of completion as if a part of the journey was finished.

Asvoria opened her eyes and turned around to see Myrrden and Jofmed one more time, but they were already gone. Now to find the one she had heard Tavol refer to as Skylar, the Ovate.

She journeyed down a path that was lined with large bushes displaying purple berries. She felt a little hungered and reached to pick a few.

"I wouldn't do that if I were you," came a voice from behind one of the bushes.

Asvoria jerked her hand back and tried to check who the voice belonged to. She could see no one and began to wonder if she was just hearing things. She reached her hand toward the bush and again the voice warned her.

"I said I would not do that if I were you." The voice sounded familiar to her as if maybe she had heard it before.

But that would be odd, she thought to herself, *since I have never been to the Druid kingdom before, nor ever met a Druid.*

She started to step off of the path but a hand pulled her back. Startled, she spun quickly to see who it was. A mid-height man, with greying black hair and beard stood in front of her. He had kind eyes that seemed to somehow speak of warning. He carried with him a tall staff with an eagle sculpted on top. The eagle held a red ruby gemstone in his talons.

"You made it past the Gates of Marana," he began, "so you must be of pure heart. Yet you lack the ability to follow simple instruction."

"I didn't read anything about not eating the berries," Asvoria said as she looked around. "Are they poisonous or something?"

"No," he said as he reached over and grabbed a handful. "They're actually quite tasty."

Asvoria looked at him with both disapproval and confusion. He chuckled with amusement. "It was just a test to see if you would heed my voice."

"Well, I don't know you," Asvoria replied in defense. "My name is Asvoria. May I ask who you are?" Asvoria challenged.

"The wise one?" the man asked. "I've only known your messenger, Tavol."

"May I presume then, that you are SkyLar?" Asvoria questioned.

SkyLar nodded and answered, "You may."

The wind blew pulling Asvoria's hood away from her head. SkyLar cocked his head to one side and with his staff, drew Asvoria's hood back. When he saw her ears, he took a step back. Asvoria quickly fixed her hood, held her body in a defensive stance and grasped the moonstone in her pocket.

"Are you Elven?" SkyLar asked.

"Yes," Asvoria said confidently and paused a second. She fixed her eyes on his with assurance and continued, "I am also Druid."

He paused for a second, unsure how to respond. He looked into her eyes and could perceive she wasn't lying. "How are you Druid?" He asked.

"All I know," Asvoria responded, "is that one of my parents was a Druid and one was an Elf. Which one was which, I don't know. I only bear the marks of both." She pulled her sleeve up and showed him the Druid birthmark. "I was raised by the Wiccans who say they found me when I was a baby."

"Found you where?" SkyLar inquired, suddenly growing very curious and uneasy at the same time, but maintaining his expression and tone so as not to alarm. He studied her arm.

Asvoria answered, pulling her sleeve back down, "I don't know. I only know that it will be 18 years ago, in three days."

SkyLar looked around him to make sure no one was near and rubbed his hand across his chin in a thoughtful manner. "It's not the smartest thing for you to come here in your situation; however," he continued, "since you are here, there must be an important reason behind it."

Asvoria chuckled slightly, "Well, I don't need to travel much farther into the kingdom as you are the one I'm here for."

SkyLar peered at her, "What do you find humorous?"

"Since last night," Asvoria explained with an expression of disbelief, "my whole life's purpose has become a rapid journey of manifestation rather than just learning and teaching. The fact that you would be the first Druid I meet and the one I'm looking for is just more of a confirmation for me, I guess."

"And why is it that you would be looking for me?" SkyLar asked.

"I am just here to ask, that you come with me to a meeting of the FLEESE," Asvoria stated.

"The FLEESE?" SkyLar repeated questioningly. "Why am I needed at a meeting with them?"

Asvoria sighed and explained, "I've seen a vision and it wasn't in favor of the Elves. There is an army of terrible beings coming against them. They will need help."

"A vision, huh?" SkyLar queried a little suspicious. "Do you claim to be a prophetess?"

Asvoria crossed her arms a little in defiance, "I'm not claiming anything. Only coming to you for help."

"Well, the Elves and Druids have no dealings with each other," SkyLar stated. "This is how it's been. I'm not even sure they will accept our help," SkyLar emphasized, "or if the Druids will heed the call."

"I know," Asvoria nodded her head. "But you are their only hope."

"Well, what of the Wiccans?" SkyLar asked. "You said they raised you. They won't help?"

Asvoria stared at the ground and slowly shook her head, "No."

SkyLar sighed and ran his hands through his hair. Then he remembered a recurring dream he had about a faceless figure calling out for help. He had dismissed it as his own guilt haunting him about something he had done many years ago. But now, it came before his mind's eye in a different light. *Could this be the fulfillment of that dream?* He wondered.

SkyLar gazed into Asvoria's eyes and could not deny what he saw there. "Where and when are we to meet?" he asked as he pulled the hood of his tunic over his head.

Asvoria exhaled with relief. "Thank you," she offered. "We are to meet at the Waterfall of Paluok in the Plains region of Enchantress Valentia before sunset today. It is where all of the regions converge so I thought it would be best."

"Well, then I guess we'd better get going," SkyLar stated. He whistled a reminiscent tune and two horses came running from over a hill. One was a luminous, shiny grey and the other was a deep red.

Asvoria smiled, "You can call horses with just a whistle?"

SkyLar laughed and said, "The Elves aren't the only ones who can speak to nature."

The horses sauntered over and nudged SkyLar in the shoulder. He patted their heads and spoke in a language that was unfamiliar to Asvoria. His tone was one of respect and endearment. The horses neighed and bobbed their heads as if answering a question.

"What did you say?" Asvoria asked in wonderment at what she was viewing.

"Oh," SkyLar said, "I asked if they would be able to get to the destination before the sun set."

"And they said 'yes'," Asvoria said with amusement.

SkyLar motioned for her to mount the light grey horse. "This is Jasper," he said. "He knows to be gentle with you." He looked at the horse and winked. The horse bobbed his head and snuffed.

"What is your horse's name?" Asvoria asked him as he mounted the deep red colored horse.

"Thunder," SkyLar proclaimed with a smile as he patted the horse's neck and smoothed the mane.

Asvoria scrunched her forehead skeptically. "That's an odd name for that horse," she said. "Why would it be named Thunder?"

SkyLar turned the horse in the direction they needed to go. "Well," he began, "everyone can hear the thunder, but it takes something deeper to hear what it's saying. Nothing runs deeper and truer then blood, which is the color of dark red."

Asvoria reflected on his comment. She didn't know why, but she felt a connection to SkyLar.

"You coming?" SkyLar yelled over his shoulder back at Asvoria and adjusted his grasp on his staff.

She chuckled a little to herself and caught up to SkyLar. Their journey to the Waterfall of Paluok was a distance away and she hoped that she may be able to find out more about the Druids. Perhaps they too were a part of the Chaos War from long ago?

~ Chapter Five ~

Out on the water, Oceanna lounged upon a bed of red seaweed that had gathered itself underneath her. She was enjoying the warm sunshine after making her morning rounds checking on all the new additions to the marine life in the oceans. It is one of her favorite tasks as Enchantress of the Coastal realm. For Oceanna, a day's duties involves keeping peace in the waters. Beyond that, she just enjoys being out in the vast openness away from the shore.

Of course, there are always times when Oceanna is beckoned to return to the coastline and tend to matters among the Elves of her realm. But that is only when Reef is not able to handle it. Reef is Oceanna's brother, appointed as her Mihman. He is known among all the elemental realms as a very strong and strategically minded Elf due to handling the dangers of the Coastal region. He excels at maintaining order exactly how Oceanna wants things done.

Oceanna's realm is that of a mysterious one named Sorithual. Located where the Raon, Leteol and Kazmor oceans meet, it's an island surrounded by the bluest waters and obscured from most eyes. The waters of Sorithual are blessed by Oceanna with a special healing quality; therefore, every sea creature finds its way here when it needs restoration.

All of the Coastal Elves wear a necklace of shells. It is their way of communicating. Reef has a special shell that channels him directly to Oceanna.

Just as she thought today was proving to be a day for relaxation, she heard Reef's voice come through the shells around her neck. "Oceanna, you're needed at the falasse of Leteol."

Oceanna sighed and slowly sat up. "What is it this time?" she asked as she dipped her feet into the water, straddling the seaweed beneath her.

"Nellethiel," was all Reef had to say; Oceanna knew right away what the issue was.

"Again," Oceanna muttered. "Where are you, Reef?"

"I'm waiting for you at the edge of the Sorithual barrier," he replied back. "We're taking the dolphins."

Oceanna sat up at attention and inquired suspiciously, "Are you on Tif?" Tif was the fastest known dolphin in the waters.

With a competitive tone, Reef answered excitedly and laughed, "Sure am!"

"Ugh," Oceanna grumbled. "Fine, I'll get Arwed and meet you shortly." She splashed the water with her hand, summoning her favorite dolphin. Oceanna pushed herself up to a standing position on the seaweed and walked in Reef's direction. The water became a solid, clear mirrored pathway under her feet. She heard the dolphin call as it jumped out of the water. Oceanna leaped onto its back, giving a command to swim, "Hepor, Arwed."

The dolphin charged ahead at an unexpected speed and Oceanna almost fell off.

"You've been training, Arwed!" Oceanna exclaimed encouragingly. "That's my girl! We may just have to put all of that training to the test."

Arwed bobbed her head while making a clicking sound to show her approval and readiness. As they sped through the water, Oceanna drank in all the pure atmosphere that the waters provided. She couldn't imagine herself anywhere else. Although Oceanna could glide through the water without feeling a drop, she loved to experience the cool touch on her skin and often would allow the water to embrace her in what she deemed a cleansing awakening.

As Oceanna drew near to the barrier, she could see Reef sitting atop of Tif. He was tall with dark brown hair. His chest was covered with a golden netting material that draped over one shoulder, which had a blue tattoo of three water drops signifying his ranking position. The netting had multiple special shells on it that were his way to contact his army factions around the waters.

Oceanna reached Reef at the barrier and came to a stop by his side, smiling big with her long braids dripping wet. Reef laughed at her tousled appearance. "You do realize we may encounter Elves from the other realm?" Reef prompted.

Oceanna giggled, "I couldn't help it. Besides," she continued in a lofty tone, "I'm not the one caught up on appearances."

"What's that supposed to mean," Reef said innocently and looked out over the water. He knew it wasn't a secret to Oceanna that he admired Enchantress Norin of the Desert Region. He also knew that, due to her disapproval, Oceanna's little jesterly pokes were meant to test his loyalty.

"Nothing," Oceanna responded, attempting to quickly change the subject. She looked towards their destination and squinted with determination. "Race you."

Reef repositioned himself on Tif. "Okay," he agreed, "but I get to say go this time."

"Nervous?" Oceanna teased with a wink.

Reef gave her a crooked smile and began counting in Elvish, "Li... mav..."Before he said the next number, Reef clicked his tongue loudly causing Tif to take off with a bounding leap.

Oceanna yelled, "Arwed, rund hepor!!" And as before, Arwed took off at such an accelerated speed, Oceanna had to hold on tight to her fin.

As Oceanna and Reef raced along the ocean waters, the other sea creatures indicated their excitement by jumping alongside them as they passed by. When the shore line was in sight, Reef smirked at Oceanna as Tif began to move ahead of Arwed, but the surprise was on Reef. Oceanna whistled and tapped Arwed triggering her to jump high in the air. Oceanna back flipped off of Arwed and skimmed the water all the way to the shore. As she passed Reef, she teasingly waved.

Once Reef reached the shore, he met Oceanna sitting on the edge of a rock, drinking out of a clam shell. Oceanna laughed and bragged, "Ha! Not only did I beat you, but I just set the longest free-foot ski record."

"Show off," Reef shook his head smiling at her.

They walked to the edge of Leteol, the one place where the desert meets the ocean. It was the most controversial point on

Erthod due to the extreme difference in regional habitat. They could see Nellethiel standing by a plant arguing with another elf from the Desert region. Nellethiel's arms were crossed and her light blue dress flowed in the wind around her as she stood with her feet in the water. The other elf, though graceful in appearance with her tall, slender figure, had her hands on her hips and a stern expression on her face. She was standing in the golden desert sand, which played an extraordinary background to her red tattered skirt and leather corset.

"Mihman Reef," a voice called out nearby. It belonged to Nihilendel, Reef's second in command. He was tall, like Reef, but had black hair with streaks of silver throughout. He had a slender physique with slight blue coloring to his skin and two black water drops on his shoulder, which indicated his rank in the underwater region.

"Nihilendel," Reef replied. "What of the situation?"

"Still going at it as you can see," Nihilendel responded as he walked up from the coastline. He bowed his head respectfully toward Oceanna as he came in step beside Reef. "Enchantress."

Oceanna nodded at Nihilendel and Reef asked, "Has the Desert Enchantress arrived yet?"

"No," Nihilendel said. Oceanna adjusted the rod that hung on her side and gave Reef a glare of disapproval at his question.

"What?" Reef asked naively. "Thought you may want to know. That's all."

"Mhmm," Oceanna responded sarcastically.

When they reached Nellethiel, they could see a dirt cloud in the in the near distance approaching quickly from the direction of Brondanum, Enchantress Norin's dwelling in the Desert Region.

"That would be her," Oceanna said as she drew in a deep breath.

The Desert Elves were known for their majestic, yet rugged and bold nature. Enchantress Norin was the true embodiment of this.

Reef stood at attention next to Oceanna and Nihilendel followed suit behind him. Nellethiel uncrossed her arms and nodded in subjection to Oceanna, which was returned in favor by Oceanna.

As the dirt cloud settled, Enchantress Norin dismounted her transport, which was a brilliant white and gold colored animal. The body was built like a horse; however, the head had the appearance of a dragon with scales covering the whole beast. Its wings were neatly tucked at its sides. A very broad and sturdy Elven guard walked in front of the Enchantress holding a spear with a rounded dagger at the tip. It was Kallo, Enchantress Norin's Mihman.

The Desert Elf across from Nellethiel bowed her head toward Norin. Norin returned the acknowledgement and moved next to her, facing Oceanna. Her eyes glanced nervously toward Reef who was watching her, then back at Oceanna.

"Ton ri dug, Enchantress," Oceanna stated respectfully greeting Norin with peace, trying to ignore the glance she noticed exchanged between she and Reef.

"Ton ri dug, Enchantress," Norin replied regaining her composure. "I understand the issue of sustainability has arose again."

"So it would seem," Oceanna answered and considered the plant on the ground. It was a small blueish green succulent with long leaves that sprouted small red blossoms on the ends. Although it was rooted in the desert ground, the plant appeared to be extending itself toward the water.

"Reef," Oceanna demanded, "Please explain the issue at hand here."

Reef motioned toward the plant with an assured demeanor and explained, "Enchantresses, Nellethiel of the Coastal region has claimed this plant needs water in order to survive. Ellentari of the Desert region claims the plant is sustainable by the watering of the desert rains in due season."

Kallo cleared his throat and stated, "One cannot deny that this plant is clearly in the Desert region."

Nellethiel turned to Reef requesting to speak, "If I may?"

Reef regarded Oceanna for approval, who nodded and Nellethiel continued, "Enchantresses, I can see the roots of the plant are in the desert, but it pushes itself toward water clearly indicating what it desires."

Ellentari was about to refute Nellethiel's statement, but Kallo held his hand up signifying for her to be silent. Norin observed Ellentari's wish to rebut and nodded for consent. Ellentari voiced her thought calmly, "The roots hold the plant's lineage. Otherwise it would not have thrived as it has. An unbalance of elemental habitat, could cause the plant's untimely demise."

Norin lifted her hand to quell the argument. "The plant knows what it needs to survive. I suggest we leave the plant to endure on its own ..." she paused and sighed, "...as I recall that we have agreed in times past."

Oceanna was about to speak, but was interrupted by a message announced through one of Reef's shells.

"Mihman Reef," a voice reported through a shell hanging on Reef's netting across his chest. It was from Kimberel, an Hethun who watched the high point of the seas for outsiders. "There is a messenger here. It is Tavol."

Reef gave an apologetic glance to Oceanna and responded into the shell, "I will be there in a moment."

"He is requesting audience with Enchantress Oceanna," Kimberel's voice relayed.

"He speaks to me," Reef declared. "Why is he requesting to speak directly with the Enchantress?"

Kimberel responded, "He said the other Mihmans had the same concern, but ultimately, it is the Enchantresses with whom he counseled. He insists that it is an urgent matter."

Norin's eyes met Oceanna's as she questioned, "Urgent matter?"

"We are about to finish up a meeting with the Desert region," Reef relayed, "I will speak to the Enchantress about it."

After a brief moment of silence, Kimberel spoke again, "Tavol would like to disclose that his message is for Enchantress Norin as well."

Oceanna and Norin exchanged a look of concern. Oceanna stated, "It would seem we have truly important matters to deal with right now other than this...plant."

"Shall he come here then?" Norin asked. "The messenger?"

"Enchantresses," Reef spoke up, "Bid him to come, but allow myself and Kallo to address him first. Just to make sure it is safe."

Kallo echoed Reef's concern, "Yes, I agree. Though Tavol is no stranger to us, one can never be too sure. Especially in an unusual circumstance such as this."

"Kimberel," Reef commanded into the shell, "Have Tavol come to the east side of Leteol. He will be met there."

Kimberel answered, "Reef, Tavol said that he will attempt his flight of travel, but he was hindered when trying to leave Ofunar after meeting with Enchantress Arathron."

Reef's face darkened with intensity as he summoned for Nihilendel. "I need you to go meet Tavol at the coastline should he encounter any trouble."

"Reef!" Kimberel shouted in alarm.

"What is it, Kimberel?" Reef charged looking out over the sea post where she was stationed.

"Tavol left, but ..." Kimberel's voice trailed off.

Oceanna grabbed the shell from Reef's hand and spoke with a calming yet stern tone, "Kimberel, this is Enchantress Oceanna. I need to know what happened and you need to speak with haste."

"Yes, Enchantress," Kimberel replied regaining her composure as she explained. "As Tavol left in his flight of travel, I saw a darkness come through the same portal but it was pulled in with him as he fled. I fear it is following him to your location."

"Darkness?" Norin repeated questioningly. "There is no darkness on this planet's surface. It was banished to the underground with the Abandoned Ones, there to remain in the Dark Crystal Caverns."

Suddenly, they felt the ground shake where they stood and

the wind started to blow furiously. A high wall of sand arose in the desert and began to quickly advance in their direction. Kallo abruptly looked at Ellentari and at his signal, they bowed low to the sand and plunged their fingers into the ground. A ripple of dunes went forth quickly across the land as the Ursav Army instantly appeared on dragons flying in from each side of the desert.

Kallo could see Ravainda, his second in charge, leading the Ursav. He lifted his spear toward the sun, using the reflection to send his order to Ravainda, which relayed that the Enchantress is on the ground! Guard and fight! At Ravainda's command, the army encircled the wall of dirt to hold it at bay.

Simultaneously, an immense tidal wave was building in the ocean and swelling toward the shore. Nihilindel ran to the coast edge and blew in the shell that hung around his neck summoning for the Jonde, the mighty army of the sea. Instantly, a hundred Coastal Elves emerged from the water with their tridents in hand. They marched on the water as one moving body, their tridents aimed at the elemental disturbance.

Oceanna and Reef ran toward the coastline to meet Tavol. Norin swiftly climbed to the nearest high point on Leteol and held her spear in the air. The spear tip became a golden yellow hook. She pointed it in the direction where Tavol was to come through.

Everything halted, even the walls of dirt and water seemed to be waiting for a command. Suddenly, Tavol sprung from his flight of travel portal yelling, "It is coming!!" Reef and Oceanna grabbed Tavol and promptly crouched down to the ocean sand.

A dark shapeless figure started to slowly emerge after Tavol. Norin focused her spear at the figure, shining a light from the golden hook, but it only slowed the figure down. The wind grew more intense causing the walls of dirt and water to tremble in their place.

Nellethiel ran to Oceanna, placing her hand on her shoulder and spoke urgently, "You need to go to Enchantress Norin! This is going to take both of you! I'll stay with Reef and Tavol!"

Oceanna immediately arose and ran to Norin's position and yelled through the howling wind, "We need to act together!" Oceanna grabbed the rod hanging on her side and thrust it in the air. The rod lengthened into a double-edged trident and she raised it in the air to join forces with Norin's spear.

"Now!" Reef yelled to them. Norin and Oceanna touched their weapons together and lightening shot forth, subduing the evil figure. The darkness evaporated. The walls of water and dirt subsided.

Reef, Tavol and Nellethiel stood up from the sand, brushing themselves off. The armies of the Desert and Coastal regions remained at attention. Kallo and Ellentari met Norin and Oceanna, then they all walked to Tavol.

"Enchantresses," Tavol said breathless and bowed. Norin and Oceanna nodded in favor toward him.

"Tavol," Kallo said, "please tell me your message has something to do with what just happened."

"Indeed," Tavol replied. "Asvoria has sent me to request that you meet her at the Waterfall of Paluok."

"Paluok," Norin repeated. "Enchantress Valentia's region."

Tavol nodded and spoke, "I will be going there next. I pray you travel quickly as Asvoria requests to meet there by sunset."

"What is going on?" Reef asked firmly. "What followed you?"

"That is what Asvoria needs to speak to you about," Tavol answered. "I'm just to request that you meet her."

Oceanna looked at Norin and spoke, "I will meet you there, Sister."

Norin agreed, "Safe and swift travel to you."

Reef turned to Tavol, "I don't think your flight of travel is safe. You'd better journey with us."

"Well, since I'm not too fond of water," Tavol sheepishly replied, "may I journey with the Desert Elves instead?"

Norin nodded in approval and turned to walk to her transport. Kallo gestured for Tavol to follow him to the waiting Ursav. He directed Ravainda, "Travel directly to Paluok with the Enchantress. I will take Tavol to his next destination and convene with you afterward."

As they walked away, Reef addressed Nehilindel who was still waiting on the water with the Jonde, "We are going to the Plains region. You will need to accompany us."

"Meurti," Nihilindel replied back. He tapped his trident three times on the ocean's surface. A fluttering occurred in the water and a carpet of manta rays appeared ready to transport the Elves to the top side of the waterfall.

Nellethiel pulled Reef aside and whispered, "I apologize for the petty matter that brought you all here."

Reef shook his head and spoke with solace, "Nonsense. What if that dark figure followed Tavol with only one region to combat it?

We saw how it took both Enchantresses to stop it."

Nellethiel nodded in understanding and turned to return to her post. Reef looked back at her. "What are you doing?"

"My position is here, at Leteol," she humbly replied.

"Not anymore," Reef stated. "I would like you by our side on this journey to Paluok."

Nellethiel bowed and continued in step next to Reef to board the waiting manta rays.

~ Chapter Six ~

As Kallo flew on his dragon over the Plains region of Enchantress Valentia, Tavol could see the exotic variety of animals roaming among the vast open lands. Among the zebras, elephants and cheetahs, he also saw giraffes, bison and gazelles. Amazing as it was to see them all inhabiting the same area in peace, he knew they were fierce protectors of their region and the Enchantress.

"We need to land there," Kallo said as he pointed to a wide prairie of tall, yellow grass with one single tree in the midst.

Tavol replied, "Are you sure it's safe?"

Kallo laughed, "We're on a fire breathing dragon, Tavol!"

Tavol politely smiled but was still a little apprehensive. His eyes were intently searching the grass for hiding wildlife that would view him as easy prey.

As Kallo began the landing of his dragon, Tavol noticed movement nearby in the grass. Kallo seemed undisturbed by the possibility of any harm. *I wonder if nature adheres to all Elves, no matter the region?* Tavol thought to himself.

The dragon landed a few feet from the tree and instantly they were surrounded by a pack of lions. Kallo remained on the dragon and did not move but rather bowed his head and instructed his dragon do the same to show they meant no harm.

Tavol observed Kallo's actions and immediately bowed his head as well, trying to calm his breathing. "What I wouldn't do to be able to use my flight of travel now," Tavol whispered quietly.

Kallo whispered back, "Haven't you been here before to relay messages?"

"I've never come into the heart of the region," Tavol replied. "Mihman Zaos always met me at the outskirts…at my request." He tried to keep his voice at a whisper but his anxiety betrayed him, causing his voice to grow louder. "You don't seem to be a bit unnerved."

"It's called respect, Tavol," Kallo replied. "As Elves, we must show it to all nature in other regions to signify our devotion."

"I just figured nature would automatically sense that in all Elves," Tavol stated keeping his eyes fixed on the animals that were gathering around them.

Kallo answered in a quiet tone, "They recognize their Enchantress and those of their region first and foremost. They are connected with them. Although I'm an Elf, I'm connected to the Desert habitation."

The lions slowly moved in closer and seemed to not be backing down. Their low growls sounded like one loud chorus echoing through the surrounding canyons. As a result, more animals started to appear and all seemed to be focused on a vicious intent.

The sound of resounding hooves caused Tavol to lift his head slightly to see an innumerable amount of rhinoceroses heading in their direction with riders on each one. Tavol knew this must be the Srinum, which are the high warriors of the Plains region.

Tavol started to shudder and Kallo reached back slowly to calm him by holding his arm. The dragon began to breathe deep, which was a sign of pending flames. Kallo patted the dragon's neck. "Hold, Yulme," he said in a low voice.

Just then, a rustling was heard in the nearby tree as a petite female Elf sprung from the branches, landing between the animals and Kallo's dragon. She held a branch from the tree in one hand overhead while reaching her other hand toward the lions. Her tan suede dress draped easily around her figure and a pair of Kamas hung on her hips. There was a look of authority on her face, yet a calming gaze in her eyes.

At once, the animals retreated and laid down in submission. The leader of the Srinum jumped off his rhino and ran quickly to the female's side.

"Enchantress!" he said warily. "What do you think you're doing?"

"Protecting my region, Zaos," she replied with a gentle assurance.

"I would have done that," he said, "you should have waited."

"There was no time to wait," Valentia said and she pointed behind her. "In case you didn't notice, there's a fire breathing dragon in my region." She moved in the direction of the dragon and Zaos reached for her arm.

"Enchantress, please," he whispered imploringly.

"It's fine," she said in a whimsical voice as she offered the back of her hand to the dragon in peace. The dragon touched her hand with its nose to denote honor. "See!" Valentia said in a cheerful voice, "we're friends now."

Valentia turned to Kallo and said with a smile, "You're welcome here, Kallo."

Kallo replied questioningly, "You know who I am?"

"Of course," Valentia answered. "I know who all my Enchantress sisters' Mihman are." She looked at Tavol and asked, "And who might you be?"

Zaos spoke up, "Enchantress, this is Tavol. He is Asvoria's messenger who has come to us often with her advice."

"Oh, yes!" Valentia exclaimed sweetly. "I've so wanted to meet you. Zaos of course would not let me." She glanced over at Zaos who was shaking his head in embarrassment. "But, it's understandable," she continued. "I know he's only doing his duty."

Tavol lowered his head reverently in her direction, "Ton ri dug, Enchantress."

"How wonderful!" Valentia stated, "You know our language. Gur throd le vegoa, teagor."

Tavol sheepishly replied, "Unfortunately, I know little. Just what I've needed." Kallo chuckled under his breath and Tavol discreetly elbowed him.

"I understand," Valentia stated with a warm smile. "I simply was letting you know that my heart is happy, friend."

"Well, thank you," Tavol answered.

"You must allow me to show you around my region," Valentia

said and raised her hands in the air and then turned around to gesture for them to take in the view of the area. "The Plains have so much beauty that you can't really see unless you walk among it."

Kallo dismounted his dragon and helped Tavol down. He cleared his throat. "Begging your forgiveness, Enchantress," he stated, "but Tavol has urgent information for you from Asvoria. And if you'd allow me to relay some recent events as well."

Zaos suggested, "Enchantress, shall I dismiss the animals?"

"Yes, Zaos," Valentia agreed.

Zaos motioned to his Left Rank Officer, Luinil. Luinil called out in a bellowing voice, "Keog thas!" ordering the animals to wander free. The lions and other wildlife that had gathered all turned and roamed away from the area.

"Zaos," Kallo said, "You may want to keep your army nearby though."

"Enchantress," Zaos asked, "do you wish to talk here or in Lujind?"

Valentia looked around and smiled, "Oh, let's just meet here."

Zaos signaled to his chief captain, Ladardyn, to hold the Srinum at watch. Ladardyn called out, "Brug ri peon!" The riders gathered the rhinoceroses quickly into a wide circular formation around the area. Some facing towards the Enchantress and some facing the surrounding area.

Valentia combed her hand across the top of the tall grass and it parted flat to the ground making a soft surface to sit on. "Shall we be seated and discuss the issue?" Valentia offered kindly as she gestured for all to position themselves on the ground.

Tavol was impressed by Enchantress Valentia. She seemed younger than the other Enchantresses but had an air of confidence about her that was striking. Her kindness was the source of her strength and yet she held an influential power that was undeniable.

As they all sat down, Zaos felt hot breathing on the back of his neck. He turned around and saw Kallo's dragon right by the back of his head. He looked at Kallo and said with a sarcastic look, "Do you mind?"

Kallo smirked, looked up at Yulme and jerked his head in an upward motion. Yulme snuffed and lifted his head up and away from Zaos.

"Tavol," Valentia stated in a sophisticated tone that impressed Tavol even the more, "what is the urgent message from Asvoria?"

"Asvoria has requested that you meet her at the Waterfall of Paluok," Tavol stated.

There was a brief moment of silence and Zaos and Valentia exchanged looks.

"Is that all?" Zaos asked. "That doesn't sound very urgent."

Tavol cleared his throat, "She has requested that all of the Enchantresses meet her there. You are my final stop."

"A meeting with all of the Enchantresses?" Valentia queried thoughtfully. "Well, this is definitely a first in many, many years."

Zaos looked at Kallo and asked, "What is it that you wanted to tell us about?"

Kallo looked at the Enchantress and bowed his head slightly

in reverence as he began, "As Tavol arrived at the Coastal region to meet with Enchantress Oceanna, there was a disturbance in the elements as a dark figure tried to enter through some sort of portal."

"Dark figure?" Zaos questioned.

"Yes," Kallo continued. "It took both Enchantresses Oceanna and Norin to diminish it."

"How did Enchantress Norin know what was happening?" Valentia asked.

Kallo explained, "They were trying to resolve a dispute over plant life sustainability between two Elven."

Zaos shook his head and said, "You know, as much as I understand the different regions and their purpose, I'll never understand the disputing."

Valentia sighed, "I as well. But, thankfully the dispute brought them together at that time to work together. I wonder why this figure tried to come into the Coastal region?"

Tavol cleared his throat, "Enchantress, if I may?"

"Of course, Tavol," Valentia replied.

"The incident in the Coastal region was not my first encounter with this darkness," Tavol stated.

Zaos leaned forward with his left elbow on his knee and demanded of Tavol, "Where?"

"The Mountain region," Tavol answered, "when I was about to leave Enchantress Arathron. I attempted to use my flight of travel, but I was knocked backward pretty strong causing me to fall to the ground."

"Did you see what it was?" Kallo questioned.

Tavol shook his head. "There was a young, female Elf named Luthien who seemed very disturbed by the matter. Mihman Polodren was taking her to the Enchantress when I took my leave."

"Did you use your flight of travel in the Coastal region when meeting with Enchantress Oceanna?" Valentia asked thoughtfully as she surveyed her region.

"Yes," Tavol said. "I knew it was risky from what happened at Ofunar, but it was the fastest way to get to the Enchantress."

Zaos looked at Kallo and asked, "Is that why you brought him here on your dragon from the Desert region?"

Kallo nodded. Zaos could see Valentia's eyes searching for significance in the situation. "What is it?" he asked.

"The darkness that is coming," Valentia slowly spoke in an assertive manner, "it is from where all darkness has been banished; the Dark Crystal Caverns."

"How do you know this, Enchantress?" Zaos asked and leaned forward a little.

Valentia looked at Tavol and said, "The darkness is using your portal to break through. Therefore, they are using the unseen dimensions, which is the only way they can leave where they have been put."

"Could there be other ways they can break through?" Kallo asked.

"I fear now that the dimensional boundaries have been broken,"

Valentia replied, "the darkness can bring havoc through other ways."

"I agree," Tavol stated. "Asvoria can explain more to you at the meeting, but you'll need to head there soon for her request was to meet there at sunset."

"Zaos," Valentia said, "please send word to all in the region to be on alert. Also, I need Ardirwen to have the Sable Antelope and my cape brought at once."

Zaos snapped his fingers three times in the air above his head. One by one, bees began to come to Zaos. They touched his fingers and then gathered in a swarm around Valentia, encircling her as she stood up in the midst of them. Tavol watched in amazement at the grace Valentia displayed as the bees paid their homage to her before carrying out the message. She then snapped her fingers once, and they all flew away spreading out around the region.

Valentia noticed Tavol staring at her and asked with a kind laugh, "What is it, Tavol?"

A little embarrassed at being caught staring, Tavol quickly stood up and felt his cheeks flush a little. "I apologize, Enchantress," he said and bowed his head in reverence. "I am just somewhat amazed that you are the youngest among the Enchantresses yet you have a way about you that appears most seasoned in character."

"Well, that's very kind of you!" Valentia responded and bowed in gratitude.

"It's time to get going, Enchantress," Zaos said standing up as he noticed the sun moving towards the western horizon.

Kallo stood up as well and bowed his head in reverence toward

Valentia, "Enchantress, I shall see you at the Waterfall."

Valentia returned the nod and smiled, "Thank you, Kallo, for bringing Tavol safely."

Kallo turned toward his dragon. Nearby, the sound of galloping hooves echoed through the region, revealing about 25 giant antelopes of tan and white color with female riders on each one. It was the Franu, which are the Enchantress' personal protectors. There was one antelope without a rider, bearing the color of a golden sunrise.

The riders stopped a few feet from Valentia. They all had light green sheer capes that draped over one shoulder and were held together by a clasp of wheat. The lead rider brought Valentia's cape to her. It was a light beige color and the tie held a small grouping of wild flowers.

"Thank you, Ardirwen," Valentia said. "Always right on time." As she tied her cape around her neck, she turned to Tavol and asked, "Tavol, will you be going to the meeting?"

Tavol responded, "I will, but only to meet with Asvoria one last time to ensure my task has been fully completed."

"Well," Valentia stated, "You have been in danger as much as any of the Enchantresses and still persevered onward with your task. We are grateful."

"My honor," Tavol said and then walked to Kallo, who helped him mount the dragon.

As the dragon lifted swiftly and flew away, Zaos motioned for the Srinum to fall in formation around the Franu. As they began to move toward the Waterfall, a breeze blew across the plains region and Zaos halted the army. He exchanged alarmed glances with Ladardyn. Valentia rode up with Ardirwen and halted next to them.

"I felt it," Valentia said. "The breeze was unstable."

"It felt like it had a strange chill on its edge," Zaos replied.

In the distance, the sound of the lions' roars could be heard. It was a signal they were in attack mode. Valentia closed her eyes for a brief moment and all waited for her command. She opened them and focused straight ahead. "There's something here," she breathed with a tone of alarm.

Just then, a lion's yelp was carried upon on the breeze to their ears. Valentia only needed to look at Ardirwen and the command was known. Ardirwen charged her antelope toward the direction of the lions and all the Franu followed in pursuit.

"We must hurry," Valentia said anxiously to Zaos, "I will not allow my sisters to be harmed in my region."

~ Chapter Seven ~

The Waterfall of Paluok was the most beautiful place on all of Erthod. It was where all elements thrived in one location. From there, the elemental regions dispersed into four directions. The water emptied from the ocean edge above that came right up against a sandy barrier. The silver mountains reached forward from the east just enough to provide a smooth crevice for the water to flow over and fall into a glistening pool below. The mountain walls created an enclosure around the surrounding area of the pool, where forest trees seemed to march from the west and take their position around the walls. Patches of slight, sandy dunes covered with desert plants could be found in between patches of tall, golden grass. It was as if the area had been strategically created.

As the Enchantresses and their armies drew near to the waterfall, they could all feel a strangeness in the atmosphere. Though they were arriving from all four corners of Erthod, a somberness seemed to have spread itself over all of the entire regions effecting everyone's emotional bearings.

When Valentia arrived at the waterfall, she quickly dismounted her moving antelope and ran to the Enchantresses who were all quietly sitting around the edge of the pool of water. Tavol was sitting apart by himself in deep thought about the day's events.

"We're not safe," Valentia said hurriedly. "There is something of a dark, unknown origin infiltrating the Plains region. It attacked the wildlife when we set our course here. I had my Franu check it out while we continued on."

They all stood up and looked around them. They gathered in closer together; their armies standing on guard in their separate factions.

"There was an incident in my region," Arathron said, "One of my Faordun saw something, well, someone." Arathron motioned for Luthien to come forward.

"A dark figure tried to pierce through upon our region as well," Norin stated. "But we fought it back."

"Yes," Oceanna added and looked at Norin, "*we* were together so I came to Norin's aide as the darkness kept pressing through. United, we were able to diminish it when it tried to advance upon the Coastal sands."

Reef aimed a smug look at Kallo across the area. Kallo just shook his head.

"Although I'm thankful for your help," Norin replied with a sarcastically humble smile, "I think you underestimated my power as I could have done it on my own."

Kallo crossed his arms and puffed out his chest in approval of Norin's words and shot the glance back at Reef.

Oceanna was about to disprove Norin's statement, but Luthien reached the group and cleared her throat. Arathron quickly turned to her and instructed, "Luthien, please relay what you saw today at Ofunar."

Luthien looked at the Enchantresses faces and suddenly became very nervous. Arathron touched her arm and said softly, "It's okay. They need to know."

"Know what?" a voice spoke from behind the waterfall. Two riders emerged and all armies focused their weapons on them as the Mihmans ran to take defense in front of the Enchantresses. There was no doubt that Reef stood above all the other Mihmans in stature and build; however, the sight of all of them together was an imposing image to behold.

Tavol yelled out, "Wait! It is Asvoria."

Everyone relaxed their stance as they waited for Asvoria and her company to dismount. No one had ever seen her before and they were all curious what this wise one looked like.

Asvoria and SkyLar dismounted their horses and turned around to see the curiosity and expectancy in the eyes staring back. Asvoria secured her hood to make sure it stayed on. She had no intention of revealing her genealogy at this time.

"I am Asvoria," she announced. "Thank you all for coming at my request." She turned her gaze to SkyLar and declared, "This is SkyLar, Ovate of the Druids."

"Why do we need a Druid at this meeting?" Polodren challenged.

Asvoria was about to answer when she saw Tavol standing off to the side. "Tavol!" she exclaimed. "I wasn't expecting to see you again."

"Well, due to some circumstances that have happened while

carrying out my task," Tavol started, "I thought it best to come and make sure you did not need anything else from me before I head back to the village."

"What circumstances?" Asvoria questioned, motioning for him to come closer.

"We encountered darkness," Tavol explained as he stepped within the grouping of the Enchantresses and their guards. "Something or someone has been breaching through dimensions, using my portal from flight of travel."

"I believe it's within my region now," Valentia said. "After you left, Tavol, we felt it on the breeze and soon thereafter, there was a disturbance among the wildlife."

"But he didn't use his flight of travel," said Kallo. "How did it breach through?"

"Asvoria," Tavol interjected, "I am remiss that I haven't introduced you to the Enchantresses." As he spoke, he graciously gestured to each person. "May I present Enchantress Valentia of the Plains region and her Mihman, Zaos. Enchantress Norin of the Desert region and Mihman Kallo. Enchantress Oceanna of the Coastal region and Mihman Reef. Enchantress Elorah of the Forest region and Mihman Dolu. And finally, Enchantress Arathron of the Mountain region and her Mihman, Polodren."

Asvoria bowed in reverence toward all of them, as did SkyLar. The Enchantresses and guards bowed in return.

"We have not had any incidents in the Forest region," Elorah stated. "We must be very well protected." She glanced at Dolu, who lifted his chin up slightly, receiving the compliment with gratitude and acceptance. As he glanced at the other Mihmans, they all gave him sarcastic looks.

"Why don't we start first with Asvoria telling us why she called this meeting," SkyLar suggested.

"Well," Asvoria began slowly and carefully, "I had a disturbing vision that I thought best if I met with you in person about. The vision revealed a great battle that will take place. In my vision, the Elves were surrounded by dark, evil beings. I've never seen these beings before, but I am told that they are evil Witches and Warlocks."

The Enchantresses exchanged an uneasy look between them.

Asvoria continued, "There's more. Some of the beings also looked like Elves."

"Elves?" Dolu repeated doubtfully. "Why would there be Elves among the darkness?"

"I'm sorry I don't have the answer to that question," Asvoria replied. "But, I've called upon SkyLar to entreat the Druids to help fight this battle with you."

"Are the Druids going to help us, even though it is not your battle?" Norin probed SkyLar.

SkyLar spoke meticulously, "I haven't met with them yet. I came here with Asvoria to meet with you all first. But the one question I have, is why would Asvoria see Elves with the evil Witches and Warlocks?"

"Is it possible that our own kin could turn against us?" Valentia asked in disbelief.

"If I may," Arathron interrupted, "I'd like Luthien to explain what she saw in my region."

Luthien bowed her head towards everyone as she started, "Today as I walked through the corridor of Ofunar, I saw Tavol about to leave. As he stepped forward in his flight of travel, he flew backwards. I saw…" she stopped and looked at Arathron who gestured for her to continue. "I saw someone standing in the portal entrance."

"Who did you see?" Oceanna asked intently.

"I believe it was one we had banished from the Mountain region," Luthien finished quickly and stepped back a little.

All eyes went to Arathron for further explanation. She quickly glanced at Polodren and began to explain, "This Elf was a powerful prince of the Highlands. However, he was found to have broken a sacred law, which could not be forgiven. He pleaded to have the law changed and when he saw that we were unbending in our decision, his heart had turned dark against us." Arathron stole a quick glance at SkyLar wondering if he knew of whom she spoke. SkyLar only returned her stare with a grave gaze.

"How long ago was this? What became of him?" Norin questioned.

Arathron took a deep breath and replied, "We banished him to the Dark Crystal Caverns about 18 years ago."

Everyone was looking at each other trying to take it all in. But glances towards SkyLar were being returned void.

"Wait," Reef shook his head and asked fervently, staring into Arathron's eyes, "you banished an Elven prince to the Dark Crystal Caverns?"

Polodren stepped between Arathron and Reef to remind him who he was speaking to.

"Yes," Arathron sighed. "We had no other way to punish his dark heart."

"But you placed him among those who have the ability to cause it to grow," Elorah stated.

"Well that explains one Elf," Oceanna said, "but, Asvoria, you said you saw *Elves* in your vision."

Asvoria nodded and said, "It would seem that there must be a plan to recruit more for the cause?"

"What was the banished Elf's name?" SkyLar inquired looking intently at Arathron.

Arathron was about to answer, but a strong wind blew into the area and all could feel a chill run through their senses. A strange feeling came upon them and their thoughts were immediately distracted by unfamiliar emotions.

"It's the darkness!" Valentia exclaimed and all armies stood in battle formation around the area.

Asvoria and Tavol started to speak a spell of protection, but all of the Mihmans and Tavol were suddenly thrown from the surrounding area away from the Enchantresses. When they tried to get back to them, there was an invisible barrier separating them. The Enchantresses, Asvoria and SkyLar were trapped on the inside. They could see and hear each other through the barrier, but it was like an unseen chasm created by an unknown power was keeping them apart.

Dark figures began to sporadically appear all around the armies.

As they struggled to fight, they found themselves warring against formless beings, as if they were nothing but air. However, they could feel the cold stings on their skin each time a being appeared. Not knowing which direction the enemy was coming from, they started to become disoriented.

"Tavol!" Reef called out, "Can you break through this barrier? We need to get to the Enchantresses!"

Tavol moved as close as he could get to Asvoria and they began an incantation in order to break the invisible obstruction.

SkyLar watched the Enchantresses as they held their heads, fighting internal battles inside their minds. He could see the light in their eyes fading, and quickly he took his staff and struck at the impediment. However, it only seemed to awaken more of the darkness now filling the Enchantresses' minds. The vibration of the darkness was as a siren in their ears. Although there was no audible sound, they could all hear the deafening effect within.

"We must come together!" Elorah instructed.

The Enchantresses tried to grab each other's hands, but it was as if they were being pulled apart by indiscernible chains. Their movements slowed as if trying to run through a vast body of water. All each of them could see before their mind's eye were dark images of fear and sadness. It was like a force driving them to turn away from each other.

"Don't let it penetrate your heart!" Valentia called out as she reached for Elorah's hand and grabbed a hold.

Elorah looked at her and drew from Valentia's strength. She took a step in closer and reached with all her might toward Arathron. "Arathron!" she yelled.

Arathron's head was down and she had to fight to lift it up. She looked at Elorah's eyes and felt her heart pump a surge of energy through her. She took Elorah's hand and turned her eyes toward Oceanna and Norin. Their backs were almost completely facing one another.

"Oceanna!" Arathron called out.

"Norin!" Valentia yelled at the same time.

Arathron and Valentia pulled in close to both sides of them and reached for their hands. Norin regarded Valentia with a sadness in her eyes that almost caused Valentia to pull back. But she pressed her body towards Norin and grabbed her by the wrist.

Norin blinked rapidly a few times and dispelled the sadness. She looked at Oceanna's back and cried out, "Sister of my heart, don't turn away from me!"

Oceanna stopped but could not turn around. "I hear you!" Oceanna responded. Since she couldn't turn her body around, she fought to take her steps backward toward the center of the Enchantransses. They began to move in towards her and encircled her with an embrace. A light shined around them, pushing back the oppressive force that was attacking them.

Asvoria and Tavol kept repeating the spell over and over trying to break the barrier. Finally, they were able to open a small portal between them thinking that they had made a way for victory, but it did not work as they had hoped. A tall, dark masculine figure stepped through. Asvoria reached for her moonstone as SkyLar ran over. But the figure spoke Asvoria's name and instantly she became limp and fell to the ground.

SkyLar ran to her and aimed his staff toward the dark figure who vanished as quickly as he had appeared. The portal closed but the unseen enclosure remained intact. Knowing that there was nothing more they could do at this point, he lifted his staff in the air and cried, "Nascmhíl! I summon you!"

A rumbling noise like thunder went out over the entire region. Great whooshing sounds were heard as the wind began to take the shape of eagles. The wind was so strong, all the armies kneeled down low to brace themselves, yet trying to catch a glimpse of the Enchantresses to ensure their safety.

The eagles of wind gathered overhead and dove toward the invisible shield with one mighty force. Everything and everyone outside of the barrier was blasted backward.

Instantly, there was silence. The wind had stopped. The evil beings ended their attacks. The barrier had diminished. But Asvoria still laid lifeless in SkyLar's arms. The Enchantresses ran over to her as Tavol and the Mihmans attempted to regain their strength.

"What happened to her?" Norin asked.

Tavol explained as he reached Asvoria's side and kneeled down, "A tall, dark figure emerged from the portal we opened. I heard it speak her name...then she just went limp."

"Asvoria," SkyLar spoke her name. Asvoria opened her eyes as he helped her sit up, but she was in a tranced state. Asvoria's hood fell back from her head and her ears were revealed.

"She's an Elf," Valentia whispered in astonishment.

"From where though?" Elorah questioned. "I thought she was associated with the Wiccans."

"I'll take Asvoria to my healer," SkyLar announced and looked at Tavol. "She'll be safe there until we can gather back together."

Oceanna interrupted, "Wait, we need to know more about how she is an Elf. What is going on?"

SkyLar gently placed Asvoria on Jasper. He mounted his horse and held onto Jasper's reigns to lead him. He looked back at the Enchantresses who were simply watching in astonishment. "I suggest you all start planning for war," he said. "I fear this was just a foreshadowing of what's to come."

~ Chapter Eight ~

SkyLar reached Wringastol by the evening moonlight and passed through the gates of the city. Weary in both his mind and body from the battle, he wanted nothing more than to rest his head, but knew there was much that needed to be done. Asvoria rode beside him, her hood pulled over her head to obscure her face and ears. She was not fully present in her mind yet. SkyLar gripped the reigns of Asvoria's horse tighter as he trekked slowly through the pathways on Thunder. Trailing through the village, he pondered the lights in the windows of the homes and buildings. The sight that used to bring him a peaceful state of being knowing all was well, no longer had that effect on him. *What a turn of events one day can bring*, he thought to himself.

He stopped in front of a humble stone building that was covered with green moss on the front side. The door had a symbol of a half-moon on it, signifying it was the healer Mirchyl's residence. SkyLar trusted Mirchyl with all important matters for they had built a strong bond. During the Chaos War, it was the two of them who discovered Erthod and led the way to safety for the Enchantresses while the Elves and the rest of the armies distracted the enemy. It was an important function of the war they fought together and they had confided in each other since that time.

SkyLar helped Asvoria dismount Jasper. As he knocked on the door, Asvoria suddenly shivered. SkyLar looked into her eyes, but still only saw an empty stare. She was trapped somewhere, but he couldn't figure out where.

The door was opened by a stately gentleman with long white hair. He portrayed a gentle disposition and was older than SkyLar, but his body still held its strength.

"Mirchyl, may I come in?" SkyLar asked while holding Asvoria's body next to his to keep her upright.

"Ovate, certainly," Mirchyl hurriedly gathered them inside, closing the door promptly.

SkyLar led Asvoria over to a chair that was situated by a low rumbling fire. The room smelled of lavender, myrrh and other spices and herbs. Shelves of books and bottled solutions lined almost every wall. A long table was positioned in the center of the room where an open book with a pair of Mirchyl's reading glasses were placed by the edge, as if just laid there unexpectedly. A staircase off to the right led to Mirchyl's living quarters.

SkyLar crouched down and pulled Asvoria's hood back, brushing her hair away from her face. Mirchyl drew near to see her face and he breathed in a low gasp.

"SkyLar," Mirchyl whispered, "her ears. Is she Elven?"

SkyLar rose to look him in the eyes. "She is half," he said.

Before he could continue, a woman with kind eyes and her hair pulled away from her face entered the room from a door in the back of the building. It was Lily, Mirchyl's wife. She was carrying a basket of fresh vegetables from their garden in the back. As she moved into the room toward the table, she could tell that she interrupted an important conversation.

"I'm so sorry," Lily stated with an apologetic smile. "I'll just put these here and …" She stopped speaking when she noticed Asvoria sitting by the fire. "Who is this Elf?"

"This is Asvoria," SkyLar answered, running his left hand through his hair and pacing around the table.

"The wise one with the visions?" Mirchyl asked with a genuine curiosity. "But you said she was half." Mirchyl reminded him. "Half what?"

"She is also half Druid." Lily glanced at SkyLar quickly in astonishment.

"An Elfid?" Mirchyl asked inquisitively. "Well, I never…" He waved his hand in front of Asvoria's face, "What's wrong with her?"

"Her mind is trapped somewhere in a dimension that I know not," SkyLar replied. "I'm hoping that you can help her."

"May I?" Lily requested gesturing towards Asvoria. SkyLar waved his hand in the direction of Asvoria, approving for Lily to see her. She walked over and put her hand on Asvoria's shoulder. "Poor thing," she whispered as she looked into her eyes.

Mirchyl looked at SkyLar and inquired, "What happened to put her in this state of mind?"

SkyLar just stared at him a moment considering how to explain the truth of the events. Mirchyl stepped closer to him and said reassuringly, "We're old friends, SkyLar."

"She requested I attend a meeting with her and the Five Elemental Enchantress Elves," SkyLar answered. "Things took an unexpected turn and we were attacked."

"Go on," Mirchyl stepped even closer to SkyLar. "Attacked by what?"

SkyLar glanced at Asvoria and stated, "I'm not sure, but I have an idea." He placed his hand on Mirchyl's shoulder. "I must go and meet with the Elders. Please do what you can for her."

Mirchyl lifted his chin a little and sighed, "You have my word." And he put his hand on SkyLar's shoulder. Lily walked to Mirchyl and folded her hands around his arm, looking anxiously at SkyLar. SkyLar gave her an appreciative smile.

SkyLar and Mirchyl nodded in understanding at each other and SkyLar took his leave. He mounted Thunder, leaving Jasper for Asvoria should she need him upon awakening. He saw a messenger coming toward him down the path and SkyLar requested him to have the Druid Elders meet in the West Cabinet right away. SkyLar didn't go straight there though. First, he had a quick stop to make at the Druid Temple library.

The pathway SkyLar journeyed on was lined with lofty aspen trees that seemed to reach toward the starry sky as if to pay homage to the sleeping sun that shined now upon the moon. As he made his way, SkyLar wondered that if his assumptions were correct about Asvoria, what it would cause and what he would do.

He looked up at the night sky and prayed, "Oh nascmhíl of the great Eagle, I pray for guidance, strength and vision as I proceed in a direction that is unfamiliar. Fly swiftly to my heart so that I may sense the beat of your spirit in every breath. May your golden beak touch my lips so they speak only words that need to be spoken in order to carry out this part of my journey."

When he reached the Druid Temple, he pulled his hood over his head and entered in reverence. He proceeded quickly to the library and located the book of recorded life. As he flipped through the pages, his breath caught in his throat when he read the date of one who was born but sacrificed, on what will be 18 years ago ... in three days. He knew this had to be Asvoria. And he knew what meaning that held for him personally.

He slowly closed the book and put it away. It had been a day of prophecy fulfilled for him in so many ways already, however, this was an unexpected discovery. Nevertheless, SkyLar knew that if this was part of a higher plan unfolding before him, he could not turn a blind eye.

As quickly and silently as he entered the Druid Temple, he departed and headed for the West Cabinet to meet with the Elders, not preparing what to say for he knew the words would be there as he had prayed. Even if he had to stand alone in support of Asvoria and the FLEESE, he would do it with all of the life that was in him.

Before he knew it, he arrived at the West Cabinet. The stone entrance that opened into a grassy courtyard was engraved with the Druid words "Go Gcumhdaí Is Dtreoraí Na Déithe Thú", meaning "May the gods guard and guide you".

He dismounted Thunder, letting him roam free in the courtyard with the other horses, their presence indicating that the Elders were already joined together waiting for him.

As he was about to walk in, he heard an eagle scream overhead confirming that his prayers had been answered. Inside the building, the walls were covered with tapestries that displayed stories of past, present and future. All things prophesied that have happened, happening now and will happen. He stopped by the tapestry revealing a great battle between Light beings and Dark beings. SkyLar had always known this represented the Chaos War, but this time he noticed something he had not before. In the center of the picture, a small figure stood in the middle of the elemental realms. He had never noticed it before, or perhaps he had but dismissed it as a representation of the unity of all realms living together on Erthod.

"Yes, of course!" SkyLar breathed, "She is to unite them in the finality of what started there but will conclude on Erthod." He patted the tapestry rapidly with his fingers as his mind raced with the new revelation. He now understood why Asvoria's life was spared the way it was, and he was free from the guilt that lay within him. But now … to explain it to the Elders.

He reached the doors and took a deep cleansing breath, attempting to release the tension from the day's events.

"Thank you all for gathering here this evening at my request," SkyLar somberly stated as he entered the room.

The Druid Elders were standing behind their chairs at a half-moon shaped table. The table faced an expansive window that overlooked the Druid lands. Not elaborately decorated, the room held only the necessary means for accomplishing decisions that needed to be made among those who gathered.

The Elders of the Druid lands were five in number, including SkyLar. Leomhann the astronomer kept careful watch of the cosmos. Fenris was a philosopher and studied the old way to link it to the new. Shulgar, the historian was an expert on the history of the Druid race and lineage from the beginning. Artaois was a strategically minded advisor skilled at keeping all things running in an efficient manner.

"Are you prepared to transcribe, Melinos?" SkyLar asked of the Druid who sat at a separate table that held a substantial assortment of maps.

"I am," Melinos replied. He was not an Elder; however, the Elders had entrusted him to transcribe all of their counsels.

SkyLar stepped behind his chair and they all recited in unity, "Beo Fada." This was their greeting before every meeting indicating they wish each other to live long among the Druids. As they were seated, SkyLar steadied himself to address the other Elders.

"Today, I was called away to a very important gathering," SkyLar began and looked around the table examining the faces of the ones who had sojourned with him for so long. "Not a gathering of Druids," he continued slowly.

The Elders exchanged looks of confusion but none dared to speak so as not to interfere what SkyLar had to say.

"It was a meeting of the FLEESE and the one who is called Asvoria," SkyLar continued and looked down at his hands folded in front of him on the table.

Fenris spoke up, "Asvoria is the one from whom we have received advisory visions, am I right?" SkyLar slowly nodded his head and looked up at him. "But," Fenris continued with hesitation, "you actually met with her and not the messenger?"

SkyLar surveyed the others who were all leaning towards him with anxious expressions. "Asvoria called a council to discuss a very disturbing vision she saw of the Elves."

"The Elves?" questioned Shulgar. He pulled his broad shoulders back and crossed his arms, leaning back in his chair.

"A great and terrible battle that promises to bring a devastating consequence to the Five Elven Realms," SkyLar stated. He leaned forward and said, "Asvoria believes, as do I, that we are needed to help the Elves with this battle."

"Help how?" Leomhann asked with a tone of sincere curiosity. "We're not strangers to war, this we all know. Are we to stand with them in this battle against a foe we don't know and who offers no threat to us?"

Artaois spoke low towards the window, "Who is the foe, SkyLar? It is surely someone of ill repute or you would not be so shaken in this matter."

SkyLar took a deep breath and replied, "The Abandoned Ones banished to the Dark Crystal Caverns."

Low gasps were heard around the table. SkyLar continued, "I know it sounds impossible and I thought so too, until we were attacked by them."

"Attacked?" Shulgar questioned. "By the banished? How?"

Leomhann scratched his head in confusion and stated, "I'm not sure what to think here. The cosmos did not reveal this."

"That is what I thought," SkyLar agreed lightly tapping the table with his hand, "until I was drawn to study the Chaos War tapestry on my way in here."

Artaois spoke methodically, "It revealed this new battle against the Elves?"

"Well, not outright," SkyLar replied, "but ... it revealed something that I'm hesitant to tell you. And if what I tell you causes me to stand alone with the Elves and Asvoria, then so be it."

"SkyLar," Fenris said empathetically, "Have we ever not yielded to your revelations?"

SkyLar chuckled to himself and looked at them, "Oh, this may cause some doubt and struggle as it did with me at first."

They all looked at each other and then back at SkyLar. He leaned back in his chair and crossed his arms. He glanced over at Melinos who was fixed intently on him.

"18 years ago," SkyLar began, "a child was born. But that child was not permitted to survive here in the Druid lands and was offered for a sacrifice."

"You speak of Reya's mixed child," Shulgar stated.

"Yes," SkyLar confirmed. "Only, that child did not die."

There was a silence in the room that was palpable. Not wanting to speak, they all absorbed what SkyLar had said. The thoughts racing through their minds were overwhelming and SkyLar could see it through the expressions in their eyes.

SkyLar continued, "That child was found by the Wiccans where she was placed that fateful night those many years ago. She has been raised by them in their village."

"Asvoria," Artaois said confidently.

SkyLar looked nodded. "It makes sense now why she would be the one gifted with visions that bear advisory messages to both us and the Elves."

"What did you find in the tapestry?" Fenris questioned.

"There's a figure in the middle of the tapestry surrounded by the five elemental Elven realms," SkyLar explained. "I had noticed it before, probably numerous times, but never understood its full meaning."

Shulgar responded, "You believe that she was saved because she serves a purpose in this upcoming battle."

"Yes," SkyLar concurred, leaning forward. "And because of what happened at the meeting today, it all makes sense."

Leomhann looked down at the table and asked, "SkyLar, does she know who you are?"

SkyLar slowly shook his head and said, "No. When I began to ponder about the possibility of it all, I kept it silent wondering if it needed to be told to her, but then…", he paused for a brief second that seemed like a hollow deafening minute to the Elders who waited intently for his next words.

"What happened at the meeting?" Shulgar asked.

SkyLar took a sharp deep breath, shaking his head. He let the breath out and conveyed, "We were cut off from the Enchantress' guards and armies by some invisible barrier. We could see them and they could see us, but," he paused, "it was a planned attack. Dark figures were coming in and out of another dimension fighting the Elven armies. The Enchantresses were fighting an unseen battle of evil in their minds. And then, one came through a portal opened by Asvoria and Tavol as they were speaking incantations trying to disperse the barrier. But, this one was not a Witch or Warlock." SkyLar looked at them one by one as he said, "it was an Elven prince of the Mountain region who had been banned to the Dark Crystal Caverns."

"Elven prince you said?" Fenris repeated inquisitively. "The Elves banished one of their own to be with those evil beings?"

SkyLar nodded and answered, "Yes. One who broke the sacred law, almost 18 years ago."

"It can't be," Artaois stated in disbelief knowing of whom he spoke. The other Elders murmured under their breath, shaking their heads.

"I know," SkyLar echoed their emotion, "he spoke Asvoria's name and she just went limp. It was then that I had to call upon the power of my nascmhíl. Then only, was the barrier defeated and the darkness retreated."

"You said Asvoria was doing incantations. Does she have powers like yours?" Shulgar asked.

"In a way. She was clearly well versed in spells but could not prevent what happened. It was just too much. She does have a powerful stone she carries with her, a moonstone," SkyLar replied. "I'm not sure what it does yet as she wasn't able to use it in time." He threw his head back to stare up at the ceiling and let out a groan. "I should have empowered the Rune of Al-giz. It was all I could do just to keep my staff vibrations focused while I tried to penetrate the barrier," SkyLar wrung his hands in frustration.

Leomhann replied, "If the dimensions were breached by the darkness, I'm not sure the power of the Rune of Al-giz, to block harmful forces, would have been enough."

"Ah, but to block the harmful force is not what it was needed for. The rune's power to stand in one's being of who you truly are without any need to fear is what may have helped," SkyLar said. "You should have seen the Enchantresses battling. I've never seen anything like it."

Fenris, nodding with his hand under his bearded chin as he listened to SkyLar, narrowed his eyes thoughtfully and asked, "Do you think he recognized Asvoria for who she was?"

"I'm not sure how he could know," SkyLar answered, "it could be simply that he recognized her as one uniting the Elves together for this coming war. See, now it all makes sense to me." He ran his hands through his hair and looked out the window. "The original war never stopped because the evil still existed, as much as we tried to contain it in one place."

"And Asvoria," Shulgar began, "where is she now?"

"She is safe," SkyLar responded cautiously. "I have her with a trusted friend. He is trying to help bring her out of the tranced state she is trapped in."

"Well," Leomhann started, "After hearing all you have said, SkyLar, I will be the first to tell you that I am with you. Erthod is our home and we should protect those who dwell in Light. Also, I do understand that the implications of this war could be just as catastrophic as, or even worse, than the one before."

Shulgar crossed his arms, "Well there are no planets left. The Elves must win this war or there will be no home for the Light to be found."

Artaois had composed himself and responded, "May this be the time to vanquish all darkness for eternity."

They all stood up and said together, "Dochas," which means to hope and bring faith in the future.

The Elders took their leave from the counsel and SkyLar closed the door behind them. He stood staring at the door for a bit, deep in his thoughts, until he heard Melinos speak.

"Is this truly our battle?" asked Melinos as he set down his pen but did not look up at SkyLar.

SkyLar walked to the window, looked out over the kingdom and sighed. "It seems to be," he said.

"But I don't understand why?" Melinos' voice displayed his concern as he looked over at SkyLar. "Why now? There hasn't been an uprising in eons of time. Then this girl comes and has a vision out of nowhere? A girl that we, *you*, have never even seen before today." His voice rose with unease as he tried to keep his composure.

"Whether we saw her or not, Asvoria hasn't led us astray with any of the visions she has shared with us," SkyLar solemnly replied. "You did not see her eyes as she explained it. Nor were you there to witness the Enchantresses being attacked." SkyLar turned around and slowly walked over to the table where Melinos was sitting. As he searched for a specific map, SkyLar looked at Melinos and stated, "She was brave to come as she did." SkyLar started to unroll one of the maps and began examining its contents.

"But why did she foresee this battle and not you?" Melinos questioned. "You are the Solitary One, the Ovate whom we trust in these matters."

"Then trust me," SkyLar said simply as he continued looking over the map.

Melinos leaned over the table toward SkyLar and whispered severely, "I don't know if I can trust her."

SkyLar regarded Melinos with a solemn expression that Melinos hadn't seen before. His gaze made him shudder, as SkyLar's next words sent a chill to his core. "You better find out if you can. And seek the strength of your nascmhíl, because if you go into this battle with any inhibitions… you will die."

~ Chapter Nine ~

The walls were moist with precipitation that seemed to always linger in the air. A twisting network of corridors and stone bridges coalesced at one gathering point deep in the recesses where countless figures had assembled. Crystal stalactites hung like daggers from the ceilings. An eerie, yellow glow seemed to pierce through the darkness in every crevice of the cavern. Pairs of blueish grey eyes could be found looking back from every point and turn.

The atmosphere held no peace. There was no love. There was no hope. No one there felt a sense of belonging, but of an emptiness. Malice and hatred fueled their existence.

A cold whoosh echoed through the cavern and suddenly before all, there appeared a tall figure with an imposing stature. His steely gray hair fell across his forehead, messily over one eye. His black sash draped from his right shoulder and around his waist. Clearly, he was revered as high ranking.

Accompanying him were ten other figures, not quite as extraordinary in appearance, but still commanding the same reverence knowing they were his elite.

Another figure moved into the space from the darkness. Feminine and sleek, her movements were heavy but determined. She came and stood before the other and they reached to hold each other's hand. Their eyes filled with a rage none had ever seen since the beginning war of Chaos. The origin of the rage was jealousy and it spewed from their beings as if it was the very life force that drove their purpose.

In one decisive motion, they raised their clasped hands in the air and every being all around them dropped to one knee. The task had been accomplished and the rest would soon come to fruition as they had planned.

"It has begun," the male figure called out, announcing the commencement of their war.

The others stood up in unison, chanting his name. Quietly at first, then louder and louder until it was all that could be heard within the deepest parts of the cavern. As the chanting continued to grow in sound, the number of beings escalated. They were coming from everywhere within the cavern until all one could see were pale eyes in the darkness resembling fading stars.

The name being chanted – Tolgin.

~ The LEE Elven Language ~

De Grodi Fab – The Uniting Call

Metasequendron – Elorah's dwelling

Besar fadu – embrace

Ton ri dug – Peace to you

O Prag – I present

Un - of

Gim hal – Calm mind

Bav ye ton – Go in peace

Funod – Thanks

Teagor – Friend

Normi – Scout

Brug ri Peon – Stand to protect

Hav – Elite Scouting Group

Meurti – to fulfil

Sleonma – Way of the Woods

Aruonta – DayRiser Mountain range

Ofunar – Arathron's dwelling

Bav rund – Go swift

Griunk – Strategic Animal Preparer

Jevas – Proceed; Continue

Fa Nuon – No fear

Faordun – Middle stage of maturing Mountain Elves

Tugeom – Mountain Region Army

Sorithual – Oceanna's dwelling

Leteol – Where desert and ocean meet

Hepor – Swim

Li – One

Mav – Two

Hethun – Sea Watcher

Ursav – Desert Army

Jonde – Army of the Sea

Srinum – High Plains Army

Gur throd le vegoa teagor – My heart is happy friend

Keog thas – Wanderfree

Franu – Plains Enchantress personal protectors

~ About the Author ~

Anita Shepherd was born in Phoenix, Arizona and has resided in the state of Arizona her entire life thus far. During a certain period of her life, she became a math tutor at a home-school group of 16 students for four years, where her interest in theatrical writing came to fruition. Anita has worked on many entertainment projects, including writing and directing plays for youth dinner theater shows as well as choreographing dance numbers for multiple venues. Being inspired by a close friend, Anita turned her first written play into a book, which later became a five book series called "The Holiday Heroes". She later went on to publish her second play as a single book called "The Holiday HoeDown". Anita's journey as an author has taken her on many adventures, leading her to write her first novella series, "The Erthod Chronicles". Her dream is to touch hearts so those hearts can touch their dreams.

~ About the Illustrator ~

Born in 1963 California, Victor has be making art all his life. He was classically trained while attending school in El Paso, TX and has followed his passion since moving to Albuquerque, NM. He has taught Life Drawing, participates in several art groups, comic cons, and has had his work hung in local galleries in and around Albuquerque, his home. While he can work in all mediums and styles of art he enjoys the open and creative genre of Fantasy, where bringing to life the creatures and characters of his imagination and those of other authors and creators.